DAVENPORT HOUSE 6

DAVENPORT HOUSE 6

HOUSE SECRETS

MARIE SILK

Cover art by SelfPubBookCovers.com/
DianeCostanzaStudio

ISBN: 978-1946413-01-7 (paperback)
ISBN: 978-09973352-9-3 (ebook)

Marie Silk Publishing
P.O. Box 873
Hayden ID 83835

mariesilkpublishing@gmail.com

Davenport House Books by Marie Silk

PREQUEL
Davenport House
Debutante

BOOK ONE
Davenport House

BOOK TWO
Davenport House
A New Chapter

BOOK THREE
Davenport House
A Mother's Love

BOOK FOUR
Davenport House
Heiress Interrupted

BOOK FIVE
Davenport House
For the Cause

BOOK SIX
Davenport House
House Secrets

More titles coming in 2017:

Davenport House
Hard Times

Chapter 1

"Good morning, dear," Clara greeted as she entered Abigail's bedroom.

Abigail stifled a yawn and giggled. "Good morning."

"Did the little one keep you up all night?" she asked, gently scooping the newborn baby into her arms.

Abigail stifled another yawn. "I wonder if I will ever sleep again."

"Don't you worry about that," Clara said, smiling at her. "I have cleared my schedule for the week so that I can stay here with you and help with the baby."

"You didn't have to do that," blushed Abigail. "I know how busy you are with the women's group. I—I am sorry the vote was denied…"

Clara shrugged. "We must simply keep trying until we get it. I am confident that we will have the vote by the next election. But we have just learned that Teddy Roosevelt cannot be our president again."

"Why can't he?"

"He has passed away," answered Clara. "Apparently, he never recovered from the malaria."

"How terrible," replied Abigail. "Who will run for office in his stead?"

"We are all waiting to find out." Clara sighed as she admired the baby in her arms. "Oh, this little boy is the most handsome baby I have ever laid eyes on. Of course, you and Ethan are both so good looking, it only makes sense."

Abigail smiled shyly. "Your babies will be lovely too, I am sure."

"I won't have children, Abigail," she replied, suddenly appearing downcast. "Lawrence has decided against it."

"What do you mean? He doesn't want children at all?"

Clara shook her head sadly. "I wish he would have told me before we were married that he did not. I don't need too many children…but I had hoped for at least one."

"I'm sorry, Clara. Perhaps he will change his mind," Abigail suggested.

Mary entered the bedroom just then. "I'm on my way to a birth," she said hurriedly. "Are you alright, Abigail?"

She smiled. "I'm alright, Mary."

Mary stepped closer to the baby sleeping in Clara's arms and kissed his soft forehead. "Goodbye, dear nephew. I would hold you every second of the day if I could." She turned to Abigail, looking at her apologetically. "I'm sorry I cannot be of more help today."

"I'm staying home for the week to help," Clara mentioned to Mary. "I will take fine care of the both of them. Don't you worry about a thing. Besides, you should be taking care of yourself now that you have a little one on the way."

Mary smiled bashfully at Clara. "I will do my best. I

must leave for now, but I am glad to know that my sister and nephew are in capable hands. Have a good day, ladies." She quickly went out the door.

Abigail frowned. "But Clara, I do feel guilty for being such a bother and causing you to miss your meetings. I have considered hiring a nurse to help care for the baby. What do you think of it?"

"Well, I am glad to help. I only worry about the expense to you, having to pay a nurse's wage," replied Clara. "I'll be as much assistance as I am able so that you may save your money."

"Oh, but I nearly forgot to tell you. The government has sent a rebate to Mary and I for allowing the Red Cross to use our house in Philadelphia. I have a little money now, and I will compensate you for having me at your house all this while."

"Abigail, you don't have to do that. I told you that I was glad to have you stay."

"Please let me pay you. It's only right, after all. Perhaps you can use the money to throw a grand party."

Clara grinned. "I suppose I could do that. Oh, it will be such fun! But I will wait until you are recovered enough to dance."

Abigail laughed. "That might take too long. Don't wait on me. Besides, if you wait too long for me, then Mary will be too far along to dance. I'll be glad to sit by and watch the splendor."

"Very well," Clara said cheerfully. "I will begin to plan this grand party. I can't wait to tell Lawrence about it the next time he telephones. It's about time we are properly introduced to the county as a married couple."

"I am glad for you, Clara." Abigail yawned again and felt her eyelids growing heavy.

"Now try to sleep, dear, and I will take this little one for a walk around the house." Clara headed for the door. "Oh, there is other news you might like to hear. Serena Valenti has returned to the farmhouse."

Abigail looked up in delight. "I must invite her to come see little Patrick! Serena was away for so long that she might not be aware I had a baby. Will you send Fiona to my room? I'll have her take a message to Serena."

"I will send Fiona. Just be sure to sleep just as soon as you've sent the message," Clara reminded her.

"I will. Thank you, Clara."

Abigail drifted to sleep after sending the message with the housekeeper. The next thing Abigail knew, she was opening her eyes to find Clara in the room beside her, attempting to calm the baby. "I think he is ready to be fed," Clara whispered, gently transferring the fussy baby into Abigail's arms.

Fiona appeared into the doorway just then. "Miss Valenti is here to see you, Miss Abigail."

"Thank you, Fiona. Please send her in," Abigail responded.

A few moments later, Serena Valenti walked into the room. She gasped in surprise when she saw the baby. "Oh, how wonderful! I am glad your husband returned from the War!"

Abigail smiled brightly. "I am glad too."

"If I knew you had just delivered a baby, I would have offered to come help, just as you came to help me with the children when I needed it."

"How are they?" she asked suddenly.

"The children are both well," Serena giggled. "They still think I am too strict with them."

"I will leave you two to catch up," Clara said wearily. "I think I will lie down in bed for a while. Babies are certainly tiring."

After Clara had left the room, Abigail turned to Serena discreetly. "How was your visit with your daughter?"

Serena looked at her painfully as she whispered, "I never saw her."

Abigail's face fell. "I thought you had been with her all this while!"

Serena shook her head. "When I arrived at my friends' house in Pittsburgh, there was a red scarf hanging on the door. I even went inside the house, although I know I shouldn't have. The family had all died there in the house. But Angelina was not there. I searched and asked the neighbors…no one knows what happened to her! I searched until I had no money left, and no choice left but to return to my brother's house."

Abigail felt painful tears in her eyes just then. "I'm terribly sorry. I can't imagine what it must be like to be separated from your child. Isn't there any way to find her?"

"There's a private investigator in Pittsburgh who I wished I could hire. He is known as the man who can find anyone. My brother has offered me all the money he has, but it is still not enough for the finding fee. Phillip will have to save for months to acquire the funds. I fear by then, it will be too late."

"How much is the fee?" Abigail questioned.

"One hundred."

"Serena, go to my armoire and bring the cash box from the bottom drawer," Abigail told her.

"I couldn't—"

"You mustn't wait another day while your daughter is missing," she interrupted sternly.

Serena retrieved the cash box from the armoire and brought it to Abigail, looking humbly to the floor. "You have already done so much for me, and I could never repay a debt such as this."

"I've intended to hire a nurse to help with the baby," Abigail said, leaning the baby over her shoulder and patting his back. "Perhaps you could be the one to help me—after you have hired the investigator—until Angelina is found."

"Thank you, Abigail. Of course I will help you with anything you need." She held the baby while Abigail opened the cash box and counted the money. "What a handsome little one!" Serena exclaimed. "Oh, this reminds me of Donnie when he was newly born. Heavens, he looks just like Donnie!"

Abigail abruptly stopped counting the money. "Does he?" she asked.

"Why yes, they could be twins!" she giggled in amusement. "How marvelous. I believe I will enjoy caring for this little one all year." Serena noticed that Abigail sat frozen on the bed, the color drained from her face. "If you still wish me to, that is."

"Yes, of course," Abigail said quickly. She held out the money to Serena. "Now go to Pittsburgh and talk to the investigator. I will tell Sam to take you to the train station. There is not another moment to lose."

Serena returned the baby to Abigail's arms and accepted the money gratefully. "I will hurry. Thank you."

Serena lived with her brother and his two children in a farmhouse near the Davenport Estate. When she returned home later that morning, Phillip looked up from where he sat in the kitchen. "I did not realize you left," he said.

"It was just for a few minutes. Abigail wanted me to visit her at Davenport House. Did you know that she recently had a baby?"

Phillip looked down at the kitchen table. "Yes."

"Why didn't you tell me? I would have gone to help if I had known. She has done so much to help us."

"How is the baby's health?" asked Phillip.

"He looked very well," Serena giggled. "What a handsome thing. Did you know that I am going to be his nurse as soon as I return from Pittsburgh? Abigail has given me the money in advance so that I may hire the investigator."

"That was good of her. How is she recovering?"

"She looked as weary as every new mother. I am only glad there is a way I may begin to repay the debt."

"When are you leaving for Pittsburgh?" he asked.

Serena was already walking to her bedroom. "Just as soon as I can get packed," she called over her shoulder. "Abigail's brother is waiting outside to drive me to the train station!"

When she emerged from her room with her bag packed, Phillip hugged and kissed her goodbye. "Be careful out there, sister."

"I will," she promised. "Goodbye, brother."

Later that afternoon at Davenport House, Abigail's husband, Ethan Smith, visited her and the baby in the bedroom, as he did every day. "Hello," he whispered to Abigail as he walked in. He observed that the baby was asleep in the cradle beside the bed.

"Hello," Abigail whispered back with a smile.

Ethan sat next to her on the bed and stroked her hair. "How are you feeling?"

"I am well," she answered.

"And how is our son?"

Abigail smiled. "He is well as can be. Just look at him."

Ethan gazed upon him proudly and smiled at Abigail. "I never thought I could love anyone as much as I love you, but I suppose I can now love two people this amount."

Abigail looked at him thoughtfully. "I wish you would stay with us here in the house. There are plenty of rooms."

"I know," he replied. "It's better this way for now. If I want to go for a ride in the middle of the night, I don't have to worry about waking anyone."

"Do you still have the nightmares?" she asked carefully.

"Most of the time I don't remember them. But Sam tells me that he can hear me from the next room, talking in my sleep."

Abigail looked down at the quilt. "I'm sorry. I wish there was something I could do."

"Just take good care of this little one. Knowing that you are here with him makes me as happy as I can be. Until I can take him riding with me, that is."

Abigail giggled. "He is a bit young for that."

A mischievous smile crossed his lips while he looked at the newborn like he was sizing him up. "I will give him a few more months then."

"You better be careful with him!" she scolded in a whisper.

"I'm only teasing," he replied. "I'm looking forward to when you'll be recovered enough to go riding again."

"I am too," she said. "Mary said I should be cleared to ride in another month or so."

"We'll ask her to watch the baby while we take the horses out then," he said.

"Oh, there is something I should tell you. Serena Valenti has returned, and I asked her to be a nurse for our baby. I suppose I should have asked you first, but it was all arranged very quickly…" she trailed off.

"I don't think I've ever met Serena, but if you believe she is fit for the job, then I trust your judgment," he answered.

"At first I wanted to ask Bridget to return and be my helper, but after what happened with Clara's husband, I suppose it can't be a good idea."

Ethan was confused. "What happened?"

Abigail cringed. "Lawrence and Bridget may have been sweethearts while we lived at the manor house, before he ever married Clara. He even bought jewelry for Bridget after he moved into this house! Clara dismisses it as a misunderstanding in order to keep the peace with Lawrence."

Ethan seemed bewildered. "Clara does not seem the type to tolerate something like that."

"Ordinarily she has no trouble with confrontation. But I believe she truly wishes to save her marriage by keeping silent. I don't want to cause any problems by asking Bridget to come back to the house."

"That seems sensible. I've never even seen this Lawrence fellow. Why is he away so much?"

"Apparently he stays with his mother in Pittsburgh. She is often ill, so Lawrence takes care of her there."

"I see. Well I hope he's good to Clara. And he better be good to you and Mary, too."

The baby began to fuss from his place in the cradle. Ethan looked at Abigail. "Should I pick him up?"

Abigail nodded with a sigh. "He is ready to nurse again. I can hardly keep up!"

"Do you need anything?" he asked, placing the baby in her arms.

"I'm quite thirsty," she admitted shyly.

Ethan rose from his seat and poured her a glass of water from the pitcher on the tea table. "I should be getting back outside to help your brother," he said, setting the glass near her on the nightstand.

"How is Sam anyway?" Abigail asked quickly. "I worry about him."

"He seems alright. He will own that parcel of land from Clara any day now. I think he is anxious to get his house built."

Abigail smiled. "That sounds like him. Thank you for the water."

Ethan leaned over to kiss her. "I love you. I'll be back to see you after dinner."

Later that evening, the telephone rang in the library. "Mr. Collins is on the telephone for you," Fiona told Clara in the drawing room.

Clara hurried to the library. "Lawrence!" she cried into the telephone. "It's been ages since I've heard from you. Are you coming home?"

"As a matter of fact, I am," he answered cheerfully. "How are you, my dear?"

"I am well, but I have been missing you. Has your mother recovered?"

"She is well enough for me to leave her," replied Lawrence. "I'm looking forward to your splendid dinners at the house again."

Clara giggled. "I will have the cook make up as many

splendid dinners as you'd like. I also have some news to share—it's about a grand ball for the county, here at our house! I thought it might be fun to host a masquerade. It will be just the thing to cheer everyone up, don't you think?"

Lawrence was quiet for a while. "It sounds expensive, Clara. Can we afford it?"

She sighed impatiently. "I would not be planning a ball we could not afford. Abigail has received a rebate from the government, and she was able to compensate us for her living accommodations over the last year."

"Well that is good news," he said. "Very well, my dear. You should have your masquerade ball if it is what will make you happy."

"I don't want it to be *my* masquerade ball, I want it to be ours. We may formally announce our marriage to everyone in the county, and remind them what it means to be merry at a party. It is our duty, after all, as the prominent family of the area."

"Of course it is," Lawrence agreed. "Should be fun."

"Then I may rely on you to stay and attend the masquerade?" Clara asked excitedly.

"You may rely on me, my dear. I'll be home soon. Goodnight, Clara."

Chapter 2

"Are you sure about this, Ma'am?" the driver questioned Serena Valenti. "It doesn't look like no place for a lady like you."

Serena grimaced as she scanned the dark Pittsburgh alleyway. She answered with a strained voice, "It is the address I was given."

"I don't like to wait around this neighborhood, Ma'am. You'd better hurry if you want me to be here when you get back. Or maybe you can try again in the daylight."

"I'm afraid I can't wait that long." Serena took a deep breath as she stepped out of the car. "I'll be as quick as I can."

She disappeared into the darkness and tried not to jump at every sound she heard from the alley. Men lay with their backs against the building—some of them sleeping—others not. The awake ones stared at her. Serena cleared her throat and announced as confidently as she could. "I'm looking for Giovanni." She felt arms grab her from behind.

"You don't need Giovanni, sweetheart," a man breathed into her ear. "You just need me."

Serena struggled from his grasp and looked desperately for the driver and the car she arrived in, which were no longer in sight. Another man from the alley approached her menacingly. "Looks like you're here to stay."

"Hey!" a gruff voice shouted from behind a door. "Get off her." The men backed away from Serena when the one with the gruff voice emerged into the alley. He turned to Serena. "I don't know who you are, but you should leave."

"I'm looking for a man called Giovanni—the investigator," she whimpered.

The men in the alley laughed mockingly. "Did you hear that? 'Giovanni the Investigator'!" guffawed one of them. "It almost sounds honorable!"

The man with the gruff voice glared at the others. He motioned for Serena to follow him through one of the doors. Serena reasoned that she might be safer with him than standing in the alley with the others. She hurried in after him.

Once they were inside, the man closed the door behind them and lit a candle in the dark room to reveal the few humble furnishings. He gestured toward a wooden rocking chair and Serena sat down. The man seated himself on a crate across from her and looked at her curiously. "How'd you hear about me?"

Serena felt her chin trembling. "Are you Giovanni?" The man nodded. "I heard people in town say that you can find anyone. I'm looking for—I must find my daughter. She is three years of age and she has gone missing."

Giovanni shook his head. "That isn't the sort of case I usually take on. Sorry." He stood up to show her to the door.

"Wait!" she cried. "I have the money just here." Her shaking hands held out the envelope to him.

Giovanni looked at her pitifully, but took the envelope and counted the bills inside. "I don't look for missing children. I usually find people who owe money to other people. I can't help you." He closed the envelope and handed it back to Serena.

"Please," she begged. "It has already been too long and I'm at the end of my rope! I'll die if I don't see her again!"

"I'm not going to give you false hope," he said gruffly. "Don't worry, I'll take you back through the alley so you don't have to deal with those characters again." Serena cried softly behind him. Giovanni turned around to look at her. Then he reluctantly asked, "How long has she been missing?"

Serena felt a spark of hope, but despaired at the answer she had to give him. "It's been at least a year. She went missing during the first influenza outbreak."

He looked at the floor. "Where was she last seen?"

"I—I'm not certain."

"You weren't with her?"

Serena felt her shoulders slump forward. "No, I was not."

"What about your husband?"

Serena took a deep breath. "I don't have a husband."

Giovanni nodded. "Because of the War."

Serena hesitated before she blurted the truth. "I was not married. My friends here in Pittsburgh raised my daughter as their own, but they passed away in the outbreak. My daughter could not be found in the house."

"Could the girl's father have taken her?" he asked.

Serena shook her head. "He wanted nothing to do

with her. He deserted me the moment I told him I was with child."

"I see," he replied. "How about any other relatives of yours? Or a neighbor of the house she was at?"

Serena breathed in exasperation. "She's not with my relatives. I questioned every neighbor for several streets but no one knew where she was."

Giovanni handed her a torn piece of paper. "Write down her name and the address of your friends. And the name of your child's father. If you have a telephone number, write that too. Otherwise write your address where I can send a post."

Serena felt her heart leap in her chest. "Then you will look for her?"

"I don't know that I can turn up anything, but I've got some time to spare…I can try…" he answered with reluctance.

Serena put her arms around his neck. "Thank you! I am very grateful!"

Giovanni stood awkwardly while she embraced him and he cleared his throat. "Like I said, I don't know if I can turn up anything, but I'll give it a shot. Write down what I told you and we'll get you back to the train station."

The next morning at Davenport House, Clara was walking toward Mary's bedroom and peered in the doorway. "Oh good, you're home," she said, entering the room. "I wondered if you will come to Philly with me today. We can talk about plans for the ball and buy our new dresses!"

Mary was sprawled on the bed and sighed wearily. "I'm very tired," she replied. "I'll wear one of the dresses I already have."

Clara pouted in response. "But it is a masquerade! You

do not have a mask yet, and how do you know it will match one of your dresses?"

Mary sat up slowly. "I'm sorry, Clara. I know how much you love to shop, but I'm exhausted. I can scarcely keep my eyes open."

"It's no wonder with how hard you've been working," Clara replied in a scolding tone. "Did you even come home last night?"

"The mother had a difficult birth," Mary groaned. "I only came home an hour ago."

Clara's tone changed to concern. "I'm worried for you, Mary. You really ought to rest more in your condition."

"I wish I could, but unless the town gains another midwife, there is no one but me. William said that pregnant women cannot return to the clinic for their births until the outbreak is over." She stifled a yawn so she could continue. "I am the only one who can help them now. Perhaps you can choose a mask for me on your shopping trip. And if you find a dress to match with a waist that is more forgiving than these awful dresses..."

Clara grinned. "I've heard of the new fashions that are coming, in which the dresses might flow with us as we walk and not constrain us so tightly."

"Thank goodness," Mary said. Then she proceeded shyly, "I left my corset at home for the last two births I attended."

Clara laughed. "Who knew that you could be such a rebel?"

"Well, it was late at night, and I was not going to wake the maids to help me," Mary explained. "William said the corsets are not so good for women who are expecting anyway."

"I agree completely. I'll see what I can find for you in Philly."

Mary giggled. "Thank you, Clara. I look forward to seeing whatever fashion you choose for me."

Shortly after Clara left, Mary was surprised to see Ethan come to her room. He knocked gently on the open door. "Can I talk to you for a minute?"

"Come in!" Mary answered in delight. "How have you been, dear brother?"

"I'm alright," he said. "But how are you, Mary? Have you even had breakfast today?"

Mary sighed. "I suppose I forgot to."

"I can get you something from the kitchen," he offered.

"Thank you, but I will go downstairs in a moment. What did you wish to see me about?"

Ethan smiled shyly and seated himself on a chair near the bed where he sat quietly, deciding what he would say. "Well, I think it's time—I think I might like to—" he stammered, "—I think I should probably learn to drive a car."

Mary laughed. "I don't suppose it would hurt to learn. It does not mean you have to give up horses altogether, you know."

"I could never do that," he replied. "It's just that I was so sure I would never resort to driving a car. I guess you could say I'm changing with the times. I want to ask Sam to show me, but I wondered if we could use your car."

"Of course," she answered. "I'm proud of you for trying something new."

"Thank you." Ethan kissed her on the cheek before he left the room. "Don't forget to eat some breakfast, Mary."

Later that evening at the house, Clara was admiring the new dresses she had purchased in Philadelphia. She heard a familiar voice behind her. "That dress will look marvelous on your figure, my dear."

She spun around. "Lawrence!" she cried, running to hug him.

He held a bouquet of flowers in his hand and kissed her on the cheek. "Good evening."

"I am glad you're here. Look at this brilliant mask I bought for you in Philly today!"

Lawrence chuckled. "I'll wear it if it makes you happy, my dear."

"It would make me happy indeed. I cannot wait for this ball!"

Lawrence set his suitcase on the floor near the bed and sat down. "Who's that fellow driving the car with Sam in front of the house?"

"I don't know who you mean," Clara answered. "I have not even seen Sam today."

"You haven't? Didn't you say you were shopping in Philadelphia?"

"Phillip Valenti drove me," she answered distractedly. "Now I cannot decide between the blue dress or the black one. What do you think, dear? I have masks to match them both."

"Who did you say drove you?" Lawrence questioned.

"Phillip Valenti, our neighbor. I suppose you have not met him yet. He chauffeurs for us sometimes." A look of realization crossed her face. "Oh, it must have been Ethan who you saw driving with Sam. I suppose you have not met him yet, either. He is Abigail's husband and Mary's brother. Sam is teaching him to drive now." Clara turned to look at Lawrence. His mood seemed suddenly changed and he stared at the floor. "What is it?" asked Clara.

He answered in a low voice. "If you need to go some-where, have Sam drive you. I don't want you asking that other fellow again."

Clara was bewildered. "Who, Ethan?"

"No, the one who took you today."

"Phillip Valenti? Why shouldn't I ask him?"

"Because I don't want an Italian driving my wife around town!"

Clara's mouth hung open in shock. "Lawrence! The Valentis are good friends of ours! Perhaps once you meet Phillip and Serena, you'll see there is nothing to—"

"Out of the question!" he interrupted. "Now Clara, remember that you already have your way with everything else in this house, but on this, I have to put my foot down! No wife of mine will have anything to do with that family!"

Clara felt tears stinging behind her eyes. "You have barely been in the house ten minutes and we are already fighting. You are tired from your journey, and worn from attending to your mother all this while. Let's not fight about this or anything else tonight. Please, Lawrence."

"I suppose we can talk about it later," he acquiesced, lying back on the bed and closing his eyes.

"Thank you," she responded softly. "I'll have the maids send up refreshments for us and we may catch up on all that has happened since you were last here."

"Very good, my dear," he replied wearily. "As long as it makes you happy."

Chapter 3

Mary giggled as she approached her motor car in the front drive. "You look like a natural," she said to Ethan.

Sam climbed out of the car as Ethan smiled proudly from the driver's seat. "Hop in, Mary. I'll take you for a spin. It's easy once you get the hang of it. Easier than riding a horse." He got out to help Mary into the car.

"If it's so easy, then perhaps I should learn to drive myself," Mary told him. Sam and Ethan quietly stared at her. "What? You don't think I can drive a car?"

"Um—it's just that—well you'd be the only woman driver I've ever seen," Sam replied carefully. "But sure, you could probably do it."

Mary laughed. "Well it was not so long ago that I never dreamed I could deliver a baby, but now I am the only midwife in the county. Learning to drive will surely be easy in comparison. Besides, I do not like to take you away from your duties so often or wake you in the middle of the night for a birth."

Sam breathed in relief. "You've got me convinced, Mrs. Hamilton."

Ethan grinned at Mary. "You'll be a natural in no time."

Mary appeared confident. "Just be sure to not tell William before I can tell him. I want it to be a surprise!"

Upstairs in the house, Abigail held the baby in her arms while she watched Ethan, Mary, and Sam from her bedroom window. She giggled when she saw Mary climb into the driver's seat while the men stood near, pointing to the pedals and steering wheel. "What do you suppose your aunt is up to now?" she cooed to baby Patrick. There was a knock at her door just then. "Come in," she answered. When she turned around, she was startled to see Lawrence walking into her bedroom.

"Hello—Mr. Collins—" she stammered. "Does Clara need me?"

"No, I just came to talk to you for a minute," he answered, looking around the room. "Clara tells me that you paid her recently for your accommodations at the house."

"Yes, I did arrange it with her."

"Now that I've come home, you can arrange it directly with me. I don't want Clara to be bothered with these things. But I do need to know if you have paid rent for your child yet. I know my wife is generous, and may have been too shy to mention that your house rent has doubled since there are two of you now instead of only one…"

Abigail was hesitant. "I only paid for myself."

"It's alright," Lawrence said casually. "I'll consider it paid in full if you give me twenty for now."

"Twenty dollars?" she asked nervously.

"Is that a problem?"

"It's just that Clara and I have not discussed it yet."

"As I said, now that I am home, I will handle these things. Do you have the twenty here?"

Abigail wanted to lie and say that the money was not in the room, but she also wanted him to leave as quickly as possible. She laid the baby in the wooden cradle and reached into the drawer of her bedside table for her purse. "Here is twenty, Mr. Collins," she said, handing him the money.

Lawrence abruptly took the bills from her hand and stuffed them into his pocket. Much to Abigail's relief, he left the room.

After he went downstairs, Lawrence crossed paths with Fiona in the Hall. "Hello Fiona. Where is my lovely wife?"

"Mrs. Collins is in the library, Sir," Fiona answered, then quickly walked away.

Lawrence went into the library to find Clara rifling through papers on the desk. "Good afternoon," he said. "Are you working on invitations for your masked ball?"

Clara laughed. "Those invitations went out long ago. I am looking for a document, but I'm afraid I've mislaid it."

"What is it? Maybe I can help you."

Clara sighed. "It's the title deed for the parcel of land that I sold to Sam. I said that I would take the deed to him today, but now I don't know where it went."

"My dear, how many times must I tell you that I will handle these matters when I am home? Wouldn't you rather be preparing for the ball?"

"I suppose I would, but if I cannot find this document, I must have the surveyor draw up another one."

"Leave it to me, my dear. Just show me the estate map and Sam's contract and I'll meet with the surveyor when I go to town today."

"That would be helpful," admitted Clara. "The parcel

is marked on the map just here. But I never had a written contract with Sam."

Lawrence raised his eyebrows. "Why didn't you put it in writing? We'll need it for our records."

"Sam is an honorable young man. His word is enough for me," Clara replied.

"Clara, this is a significant transaction, not some confirmation to attend a party. It really should be in a written agreement."

"I know," she sighed. "But the thing is, Sam can't read. I don't see how much good it would do to put it in writing anyway."

Lawrence was quiet for a moment, then looked up at Clara. "Go see to your party arrangements, my dear. Leave the matter of the land to me."

"Thank you," she breathed in relief, moving away from the desk so that Lawrence could sit down. She hugged his shoulders and kissed his cheek. "It's good to have you home again."

Later that afternoon, Sam timidly entered the library where Lawrence was waiting for him. "You wanted to see me, Mr. Collins?"

"Come on in, Sam. I understand you've been waiting for that document from my wife."

Sam approached the desk and stood there awkwardly. "That's right, Sir."

Lawrence held out a paper to Sam. "Have a look at this and see that everything is in order."

Sam took the paper from him and stared at it blankly for a few moments. "Uh—yes Sir—everything seems to be in order."

"Very good," replied Lawrence, handing a pen to Sam.

"Then sign both of these papers. One is for my records and the other is for you to keep."

Sam took the pen from Lawrence and drew an "X" on the papers as he had learned to.

"It's a pleasure doing business with you, Sam," Lawrence told him as he filed one of the papers in the desk drawer.

"Yes Sir," Sam replied. He left the library with the document in his hand.

Later that evening at the Valentis' farmhouse, Serena was just returning from her trip to Pittsburgh. Phillip looked at her expectantly when she walked through the door. "We're just about to have supper. How'd it go?"

Serena looked weary but still seemed hopeful. "I spoke to the investigator. He is called Giovanni and he will search for Angelina. I think he will find her."

"The investigator was optimistic, then?"

"I have a good feeling about him," she replied. "There was something in his eyes that told me he will not give up until he finds her."

"Then we will pray for his search," Phillip told her. He turned to the two young children who were playing in the room. "Gabriella, Donnie, go wash up for supper and set an extra place for your Aunt Serena." The children obeyed, leaving for the washroom.

"I'm going to pay a quick visit to Abigail so I can tell her that I met with the investigator. She will be glad to see that I am back so I may begin helping with the baby." Serena paused thoughtfully. "It's the most curious thing—Abigail's baby reminds me of Donnie when he was newly born. The baby looks just like him!"

Phillip rose from his seat and carried a baking dish to the table. "I suppose all babies look alike," he mumbled.

Serena laughed. "I suppose they do, but the resemblance is almost startling. Maybe if you saw him, you would see what I mean."

Phillip shrugged and began re-arranging the plates at the table. Gabriella and Donnie returned to the kitchen, and Serena hurried out the door on her way to Davenport House.

Abigail was having dinner at the tea table in her bedroom with Ethan sitting across from her. Ethan stood up when Serena knocked on the open door. "Serena," Abigail greeted cheerfully. "You look well! Please allow me to introduce my husband, Ethan."

Serena gave a shy smile. "Good evening, Mr. Smith."

"Miss Valenti," he greeted with a nod.

"Abigail, I want you to know that the trip to Pittsburgh was a success. I think I will hear news of the search very soon."

"Oh, I hope so," Abigail replied kindly.

"Would you like me to stay with the little one tonight?" she asked.

"I think I we'll be alright for now, but perhaps you have heard of Clara's masquerade ball. I hoped you might care for the baby that evening, so that I may attend the ball with my husband. Could you arrive at 6 o'clock on Saturday?"

Serena nodded. "I am grateful to you for arranging it with me."

"And I will be grateful for your help. I wished to hire a nurse who I could trust with the baby, and I believe you are the perfect person."

"Thank you, Abigail. I don't want to interrupt your meal. I'll return on Saturday at 6 o'clock sharp."

After speaking to Abigail, Serena headed down the

stairs to the front door. Clara and Lawrence were on their way to the dining room and nearly ran into Serena in the Hall. "Good evening, Serena," Clara greeted in surprise. She turned to Lawrence. "May I present my husband, Lawrence Collins. Lawrence, here is our neighbor, Serena Valenti."

Instead of greeting Serena, Lawrence turned angrily to Clara. "I thought I made myself clear. I don't want her kind anywhere near the house!"

Clara's cheeks burned in embarrassment. She looked apologetically at Serena, who appeared just as mortified, cowering under Lawrence's glare.

Serena turned to look at Clara. "I was just leaving," she whispered hoarsely. She stepped around them and hurried out the door.

"Lawrence, how could you?" Clara fumed. "I've never been so humiliated in all my life!"

"It was you who invited her into the house just to vex me, when I told you to have nothing to do with them!"

"I did not invite Serena tonight, but even if I had, the least you could do is be civil! I'm going to take dinner in my room. I will not dine with you tonight after all!" Clara stormed up the stairs, her tears blinding her. She slammed the door when she got to her room.

Ethan and Abigail heard the shouting voices from downstairs and looked at each other with wide eyes. "Is it always like that when he comes home?" Ethan asked about Lawrence.

"It seems to get worse every time," she admitted, and rose from her seat to close the bedroom door. "Ethan, something happened today. Lawrence came into my room demanding that I pay rent for two, now that the baby is here."

"What? Lawrence came here into your bedroom? Was Clara with you?"

Abigail shook her head. "I was alone with the baby and it was all very awkward. Lawrence said that he handles the money while he is home, and that I should give him twenty dollars because the baby lives here now."

"Twenty dollars is ridiculous," Ethan said. "But I especially don't like that he was here alone with you. He should know better than to enter a lady's bedroom."

"I did not like it either, but I was caught off-guard. I intend to keep my door locked from now on."

"I'll have a word with him," Ethan said. "I don't care if we haven't been properly introduced yet."

"Oh please don't, Ethan. I don't want to make things more uncomfortable with him than they already are."

"He shouldn't be bothering you, Abigail. You should be able to feel comfortable here without worrying about the door being locked."

"It is only until the Red Cross is through with our house," Abigail said. "Then we can move back and not worry about such things. I might speak to Clara about the twenty dollars once the masked ball is over. I don't believe she is aware that Lawrence asked me for the money, but I also don't wish to cause strife when she is occupied with the party and already on thin ice with Lawrence."

Ethan moved his chair beside her and held her hand. "I'm going to bring a pot of strong coffee so I can stay with you tonight. I won't go to sleep, I'll just stay by your side and look after you and the baby."

Abigail's heart fluttered at his touch. "But when will you sleep?"

Ethan leaned toward her and kissed her face. "Don't

worry about me. What's important now is that you feel comfortable. If anyone tries to bother you, they'll have me to contend with."

At the Valentis' farmhouse, Serena stumbled through the door of the kitchen where Phillip and the children were waiting to eat their supper. Phillip had a sinking feeling when he saw that his sister was pale and seemed distressed. "What is it?" he asked.

Serena shook her head and walked past the table. "I won't be working in that house after all," she replied, her voice catching in her throat. "Go ahead and eat without me." Serena went to her room and closed the door behind her.

The children looked up at their father and he nodded at them to begin eating. Then he rose from his seat and went to Serena's door. "What's going on?" he called through it.

"I won't speak of it, brother," she answered from the other side.

Phillip clutched his chest in fright. "Did something happen to the baby?"

Serena hesitated before she answered. "The baby is fine. I just don't want to face Clara again."

Phillip breathed in relief and said, "I'll set aside a plate of supper for you." He returned to his chair at the table and the children looked at him curiously.

"Are you alright, Papa?" Donnie asked.

Phillip looked at his plate and twirled his fork through the pasta. "I'm alright, Donnie."

Chapter 4

Ethan felt his eyelids growing heavy while he sat in the rocker near the fireplace. He decided to leave his seat and pour himself another cup of coffee. When he set the pot back on the tray, the baby began to stir from his sleep. Ethan cringed, hoping that the little one might fall back asleep. But when the baby continued to stir, Ethan took him in his arms and returned to the rocking chair so they would not wake Abigail. He held the baby to his chest and leaned against the back of the chair, reminding himself not to drift to sleep. He looked down at the baby's head and smiled as he stroked the soft hair.

"It's the most lovely feeling, isn't it?" Abigail whispered from the bed.

Ethan looked at her apologetically. "I must have woke him when I poured my coffee. How do I get him to go back to sleep?"

Abigail giggled. "He won't go back to sleep until I feed him. He usually wakes up around this time."

"He eats during the night too?" Ethan asked incredulously.

"Why do you think I look so tired all the time?" she

replied with a wry smile. "It's why I wanted to hire a nurse to help me during the day."

Ethan nodded. "Makes sense."

"Since we are both awake, maybe we can discuss something I've been meaning to bring up. I have spoken to Father Salvestro, and he agreed to have a christening ceremony for us at his home. It would be safer than traveling to the city church while the influenza is widespread."

"Alright. When will the christening be?" asked Ethan.

"I'd like to have it before we move to the manor house. Perhaps this spring?"

"Whatever you think, Abigail. I don't know much about how this stuff works."

"It's why I hoped we could talk about it. During the christening, we may name who Patrick's godparents should be."

"I'm sure it will be Mary and William."

Abigail smiled shyly. "I would choose Mary and William as well, of course, but they are not Catholic. They could not be named as godparents for the christening."

Ethan looked confused. "Then who were you thinking about?"

"Well, I thought maybe we could ask Sam to be godfather. What do you think?"

Ethan shrugged. "I suppose we don't have much choice."

Abigail laughed. "You don't sound convinced. I'll wait to say anything to him until you are certain." She propped the baby up to her shoulder and patted his back while Ethan yawned and closed his eyes. "Why don't you go to bed now? I will likely stay awake anyway to work on the christening gown."

Ethan opened his eyes with a start, embarrassed that he

had already begun to drift to sleep. "Are you sure? I can stay if you need me."

"You're already falling asleep now," she giggled. She laid Patrick on the bed and went to Ethan to kiss his cheek. "I think we will be fine. Now go to bed and dream about how much you miss me."

Downstairs in the servants' quarters, Fiona addressed the staff at the table while the maids were beginning their breakfast. "Miss Clara tells me that the ballroom has not been used for many years, but of course that will all change on Saturday. Nora will work on the cleaning and polishing while Jane attends to the rest of the house."

The servants' door to the outside suddenly swung open. Fiona rose from her seat to see who was there and then tried to hide her astonishment. "Mr Collins—good morning," she stammered.

Lawrence looked around the room. "I didn't think anyone would be awake yet."

"We've just begun our day, Sir. How may I help you?"

"I need a place to store these," he said, pointing to the crates being unloaded from a carriage by two men. They were labeled as boxes of wine and spirits.

"Oh—certainly," Fiona replied. She led him to the wine cellar.

"I don't want to store them here," Lawrence frowned. "Where else can we take them?"

"There's a storage room just near the laundry…" she said uncertainly.

"Right. Take me to that one."

Lawrence seemed satisfied when Fiona showed him the storage room. He went back outside and directed the men to stack the crates in the room. Fiona stood by and watched with wide eyes. Lawrence winked at her. "We're about to have a party, aren't we? Might as well make it a great one before they make this stuff illegal."

"This wine is for the party?" Fiona questioned.

"Well, not all of it," he laughed. "Here, you can start with this one on Saturday night. We won't serve the good stuff 'til last."

Fiona nodded. "Of course, Sir."

Later that morning, Fiona was delivering the post to Clara in the library. Clara seemed pleased about the tall stack of letters and she opened them quickly. "Nearly everyone in the county will be attending the ball," she said proudly. "I had no idea so many would respond! I suppose everyone is eager to take part in something cheerful again. Now remember, Fiona. This party must go perfectly. It will be the official introduction of Lawrence and I as a married couple. I am counting on you to ensure that it all runs flawlessly."

"Of course, Miss Clara," she answered solemnly. "Nora is polishing the ballroom today and Mrs. Malone has been preparing the party food nonstop. There is one matter that I wanted to discuss…Mr. Collins has given instructions for the party drinks—"

They were interrupted by Lawrence walking into the library. Clara's mouth was open in surprise. "Lawrence, I'm delighted that you are taking part in planning the ball! Fiona said you have instructions for the drinks?"

"I explained it to her this morning, my dear…if it is alright with you of course," he replied.

"I'm certain whatever you have planned will be fine," Clara said, nodding to Fiona.

"Very good, Miss Clara," Fiona said, then left the library.

Lawrence sat down at the writing desk and pulled some envelopes from his pocket. Clara looked at him curiously. "Did the post come again?" she asked, peering at the letters. "I hope they are more responses for the party."

"No—these letters are for me," Lawrence stuttered.

Clara frowned when she saw the address on the top letter. "You still receive mail in Pittsburgh? Why not have it directed to our house?"

"I still have it delivered to my mother's house since I am there so often. I just haven't bothered to forward it yet."

Clara continued to stare at the envelope but Lawrence abruptly moved it from her view. "It is nothing to bother you with, my dear. Just business."

"I wish you would have your mail sent here. It hardly feels as though we are married, and it's been over a year."

"I'll inform the post office, my dear, if it will make you happy," he said, stuffing the letters back into his pocket. "Now I really must be leaving. I'll catch up with my correspondence later."

"Leaving?" she questioned in disappointment. "Where do you need to go today?"

"Philadelphia."

"But you will be back in time for the masquerade?" she prodded.

Lawrence chuckled. "Of course I will be here, my dear. I know how important it is to you. I will only be in Philly for a day. Then I'll be home with plenty of time to spare." He kissed her on the cheek and headed out the door.

Clara sat at the desk in the library while a strange feeling settled over her. She took out a paper and wrote down the address she had memorized from Lawrence's letter, then sat there quietly contemplating what she might do with it.

Ethan walked into the library and saw Clara staring blankly at the desk. "Oh, I didn't know anyone was in here," he said, turning to leave.

"You don't need to go, Ethan. I'm just thinking."

Ethan could tell that she was upset. "Is everything alright?"

"I don't know if everything is alright or not."

"Can I help?" he asked. Clara continued to stare blankly. Ethan continued in a quiet voice, "I'm sorry you're not happy with him."

Clara looked up at Ethan. "Is it that obvious I'm unhappy? I suppose such a thing is not possible to hide forever."

"He should be good to you, Clara. You deserve to be treated decently."

Clara forced a smile. "It means a lot to hear you say that. Thank you."

"You helped me at a time that I needed it, and I want to help you if you need me," he responded. Ethan walked by the bookshelves with his hands in his pockets, browsing the selection.

Clara was quiet for a long while and finally decided to change the subject. "Do you have a mask for tomorrow night?"

Ethan remained facing the bookshelf. "Mary picked up some masks in town for me and Abigail, but…" he hesitated. "I don't know if I'll be at the party."

"What do you mean? Where will you be?"

He still would not face her when he replied. "I don't want to be here with Valenti. I'm sure you invited him."

Clara had a sinking feeling. "I suppose I did invite him. Should I not have? I'm sorry."

"You should invite whoever you want to your house. It's just hard for me, that's all."

"I suppose I was not thinking of—whatever you might think about it," she said apologetically.

"It's strange, really. I thought of him like a brother during the war. The last thing I expected was to come home to him married to my wife."

"I know it was a shock," Clara said quietly. "I should have been more considerate when I made out the invitations. I'll be more aware in the future."

Ethan turned around to face her, his voice catching with emotion. "You don't need to do anything special on my account. Abigail and I will be going back to the manor house soon anyway. Maybe you shouldn't tell her what I said about the party. I don't want Abigail feeling bad for anything. I feel bad enough for the both of us." He turned around and left the library empty-handed.

Clara looked after Ethan sadly as he walked away. Then she turned her eyes to the paper she had written the address on. She took the paper and left the library, gathered her coat and hat from the hall closet, and walked next door to the Valentis' farmhouse.

" 'Morning," Phillip greeted her at the door.

"Good morning," she said quickly, and held out the paper for him to see. "Can you take me to this address?"

Phillip raised his eyebrows. "I know right where it is. I used to live by this street, but it's a long drive. Do you plan to stay in Pittsburgh overnight?"

"Would I have to? Or can we be there and back in a

day? I just need to check on something. I don't imagine it will take too long."

"Sure, I could have you back to the house tonight, but it will be late. Let me just tell Serena that I'm leaving."

"Very good," nodded Clara. "I'll be waiting in the car."

They drove for hours to reach Pittsburgh. When Phillip parked the car at their destination, Clara stared curiously at the house that matched the address from Lawrence's mail. "I'll just be a moment," she told Phillip as he helped her out of the car. Clara approached the house nervously, her heart sinking every step of the way, knowing that something was wrong. When she knocked on the door, a middle aged man answered. "Um—good afternoon," Clara stammered. "I wonder if I might visit with Mrs. Collins—if she is well enough to receive me."

The man seemed irritated when he answered her. "There ain't no Mrs. Collins living here. If you want to see Lawrence Collins, you just missed him."

"Lawrence was just here?" Clara asked incredulously. "But, his mother does not live here in the house with him?"

The man shrugged. "Look, lady, this is my house, but Lawrence rents one of the rooms from me. I think his ma died a long time ago."

Clara felt her knees going weak. Her head spun with confusion. Phillip became concerned as he watched from the car, and he reached Clara just in time for her to hold onto him for balance. "Take me home, quickly," she whispered.

Phillip helped her to the car. "You don't look well. Is there anything you need?"

Clara shook her head in bewilderment. "I've had a terrible feeling that Lawrence was hiding something from me…now I'm too afraid to find out what it is. I just want to go home." Phillip started the car and they began the long drive back to Davenport House.

In the servant's quarters, Fiona was instructing the maids on the proper order to serve the wine for the party. The masquerade preparations were nearly complete, and Fiona left the house to breathe in the fresh air. Sam observed that she was sitting on the boulder near the servants' entrance and he went to talk to her.

"Do you have a minute?" he asked cheerfully. "There's something I want to show you."

Fiona smiled wearily. "It's been a long while since I had a break. What do you want to show me?"

"I have to get it from my room," he replied. Fiona followed him to the stable and waited outside while Sam went to the apartment above. He soon returned with a document. "I've got the deed to my land now. I can start building anytime!" He held it out to her proudly.

Fiona gasped in delight. "How wonderful! You have worked hard for it—" she stopped suddenly. "Oh—Sam, this is not the deed. Perhaps you brought back the wrong document." She held it for him to take back.

Sam furrowed his brow. "That's supposed to be the deed. Miss Clara said I was done working and paying for it."

Fiona skimmed it over. "Miss Clara gave this to you?"

"It was Mr. Collins who gave it to me. He said I should sign it."

Fiona had a sinking feeling. "Are you certain Miss Clara said you completed the payments?"

"Of course I'm sure," he said, getting flustered. "Fiona, what does it say? You've got me worried now."

"It's a contract," she answered slowly as she continued to read. "But it says you've agreed to work another year in payment for the land."

Sam was aghast at first, then he clenched his fists in anger. "It can't be! Miss Clara said that I was done! Why would she give me this contract after all that?"

"The contract is not written in Miss Clara's hand. I'm afraid there was a misunderstanding when Mr. Collins gave this to you. Either that, or…he has tricked you."

"Why would he do that?"

Fiona looked around her, then lowered her voice to a whisper. "I shouldn't be saying this, but Mr. Collins is not a good man. If you only knew what he was like in the house…I only feel safe when he is away."

His face turned red with anger. "Has he bothered you?"

"Not exactly," she sighed. "But he proposed something shameful to Bridget."

"Your sister?" Sam asked incredulously.

Fiona nodded. "As I said, he is not a good man." She held the contract out to Sam. "This is just the sort of trick I think he would do. Miss Clara's name is not on the contract—she may not know that he made you sign this."

"Then I'll talk to her," he said.

"She is not home now…neither is Mr. Collins. But Sam, won't you wait until after the masked ball? I worry about what problems it might cause while Miss Clara is organizing the event."

Sam was reluctant. "It seems like the sort of thing that should be cleared up right now. I can't let her think I agreed to this."

"I know that," Fiona said with pleading eyes. "But

everyone has been on edge lately at the house. I think they will begin to relax once the ball is over."

"Fine, I'll wait," he acquiesced. "But I don't like this Mr. Collins fellow one bit. He's going to pay for what he's done, one way or another."

* * *

*Temporary Red Cross Hospital at Smith
Manor House, Philadelphia*

"Nurse Miller, will you go outside and see what that young man wants?" the director asked, pointing out the window to the man with a messenger bag who was waiting outside.

"Right away," answered Bridget. She hurried outside to meet the young man, and noticed that he was missing an arm where his coat sleeve hung loosely. "Do you need help getting inside the hospital, Sir?"

"Oh, hello," he said distractedly, looking at the house as he spoke. "No, I don't need to get inside. I didn't realize this house would be a hospital now."

"It is," she replied. "Do you have a delivery for the family who used to live here?"

"You know them?" he asked.

"I used to work here as a maid for the family. Now I am here as a nurse with the Red Cross."

"I see," he said, squinting his eyes curiously. "Is your name Bridget, by any chance?"

Bridget laughed nervously. "How do you know my name?"

The man sighed like he was exasperated all of a sudden.

"I don't suppose you remember a man called Lawrence Collins? He used to have this route."

Bridget felt her stomach twisting into knots at the mention of his name. She swallowed hard before answering in a low voice. "I remember him."

"Believe me, you're better off to be rid of that fellow," the man said, shaking his head.

"What do you mean?" she demanded, feeling uncomfortable that this stranger seemed to know so much about her.

"I used to work with him at the post office. Lawrence would come in to work and brag about seducing you. He said he was only getting information from you so he could trick the rich lady you worked for. Lawrence thought he could get the lady's house and money that way."

Bridget felt anger rising through her. "What a rude thing for you to say! What's the point of telling me this now?"

"Sorry, Miss. I thought you'd feel better if you knew what a scoundrel he was. He dodged the draft, you know. He was a real coward…I hope the rich lady is alright and didn't fall for his tricks."

"You're too late. They were married over a year ago," she said coolly, crossing her arms over her chest.

"It's a shame," the man replied, bowing his head sorrowfully. "That poor lady must have truly been widowed from the War. I suppose it happened a lot."

"I don't understand what you mean. Clara was never married before she met Lawrence."

"Who?"

Bridget sighed impatiently, beginning to believe this young man did not know as much as he thought he did.

"Clara Davenport. Lawrence's wife. Now she is Clara Collins, obviously."

The man looked at her skeptically. "That's not what Lawrence called her. Are you sure that he married a lady named Clara?"

Bridget rolled her eyes, becoming more angry every moment she had to talk about Lawrence. "Of course I'm sure! I know everything about Clara, and I know everything about the family and Davenport House! Now if you don't have anything important to say, please go away and don't come back." She turned her face away from him.

The man sighed. "I'm sorry I bothered you, Miss. I never heard of this Clara Davenport lady or her house before now. Lawrence talked about a scheme he had for a different lady. It really was despicable…I'm glad he never went through with it. He bragged that he knew someone at the war office who would send a false death note about the lady's husband. Lawrence said he could trick her and take her money. I wanted to warn the lady, but I got called to fight and didn't get back 'til now. I suppose the lady must have been your Mistress. Lawrence said her name was Abigail. Abigail Smith."

Chapter 5

The following afternoon, Phillip walked out to the orchard behind the farmhouse to find Serena. "Something came in the post for you."

"Where is it?" she cried.

"I left it on the mantle."

Phillip followed Serena inside the house where she took the envelope from the mantle and tore it open.

Miss Valenti,

Your daughter is alive and well. I can't get her from where she is yet. I'll write again when I find a way.

Giovanni

Serena felt her heart racing in her chest. "I don't understand," she said, her voice shaking. "Giovanni writes that he found Angelina, but that he can't get to her. What do you think it means?" She handed Phillip the letter.

Phillip looked it over and frowned. "He probably wants more money."

"If he wanted more money, why didn't he just say so in the letter?" Serena lowered herself into a chair at the kitchen table. "At least he found her...and she is well."

Phillip looked at her skeptically. "What was all that business about you not working for Abigail anymore? How will you repay your debt to her?"

Serena looked down at the table. "I'll find a way to pay her...but it can't involve me returning to the house."

"What happened? Why don't you want to go back?"

Serena shook her head. "You'd be furious if I told you."

Phillip was bewildered. "Why would I be furious? I'm only concerned that Abigail is rightly paid. It's ungrateful of you to back out of the arrangement you made with her, after all she's done for you."

"I'm not ungrateful, brother. Abigail has done more for me than only the hundred dollars could repay. You must believe me that I'm burdened with a terrible guilt that I won't help her as I promised."

"You'll at least explain to her, I hope...since you will not explain it to me," Phillip told her.

Serena looked up at him. "Don't you see? I can't go back into that house! Not even to explain. I was forbidden!"

Phillip was getting impatient. "By who, Clara? Is she shunning you because of Angelina?"

"She doesn't know," Serena answered, returning her gaze to the table. "At least, I don't think she knows. But if I tell you the true reason, you must promise not to interfere in any way."

"What does any of this have to do with me? Just tell me, Serena. I don't even go into that house anymore."

Serena swallowed the lump in her throat. "I can't go back because…Clara's new husband…he is Angelina's father."

Serena watched her brother's face turn red with anger and he balled his fists at his side. "I'm going to kill him," he growled.

"Now you see why I didn't want to tell you!"

Phillip breathed angrily through his nostrils. "I can't believe that the coward who left you is the man who lives next door! How could you not tell me?"

"I never knew until that night I went to the house and Clara introduced us. When I saw it was Lawrence, I nearly fainted! He stopped me after I left the house. He said that he knows where Angelina is, and if I go to the house again or if Clara finds out anything, he'll see to it that I never find her!"

"All the more reason for me to hate him," Phillip seethed. "The girls must be told. They need to know what sort of lowlife is living in their house!"

"Don't you dare say anything until my daughter is safely back with me," she said firmly.

He plopped down with a scowl in one of the chairs. "I don't like this one bit, knowing he's there…in the house with them. Once your investigator gets Angelina, Lawrence is going to get what he deserves from me."

At Davenport House, the maids were hurriedly making last minute preparations for the ball. Clara was frantic in the drawing room, asking Fiona again and again to be sure that the party would run perfectly. When they heard someone knocking at the door, Clara's eyes grew wide. "Who on earth could that be? The party does not start for hours, and I'm a mess!"

Fiona quickly answered the door and returned to the drawing room to inform Clara. "Mr. Blake is here to see you."

Clara smoothed her hair and dress. "Send him in, Fiona."

When Clara saw her neighbor, Joe, she felt her heart race in her chest. He was the man who worked on the ranch next to the Davenport Estate, and he was looking as tan as ever. Clara had to suppress the feelings that arose whenever he came near. "Mr. Blake, how good to see you," she greeted. "You're coming to the ball tonight, aren't you?"

Joe chuckled nervously. "Well that's the thing, Mrs. Collins. I appreciate the invitation, but I um—I don't have a mask—so I won't be coming. I'm sorry I forgot to send the card back. I figured I could come tell you in person."

Clara shook her head dismissively. "Wait a moment, and I will get a mask for you. I purchased extras in case anyone came without."

"You don't have to—" Joe began. But Clara had already left the drawing room.

She returned with a black mask that tied around the back. "Here you are, Mr. Blake," she said, looking at him with pleading eyes. "Now may we expect you tonight?"

Joe smiled timidly as he took the mask, feeling too guilty to refuse. "Sure, I'll be here."

Clara sighed in relief. "Thank you."

"I'll see you tonight then, Mrs. Collins. Good day," Joe said, then he left for the door.

Clara and Fiona began to discuss the placement of the orchestra in the ballroom. When there was another knock at the front door, Clara turned to Fiona in exasperation. "Who can that be now? I hope Mr. Blake has not changed his mind."

Fiona went to answer the door and gasped at the sight of her sister on the other side. "Bridget? What are you doing here?"

"I need to speak to Clara…about Lawrence," Bridget replied. "It's urgent."

Fiona's eyes grew wide. "I don't think that's such a good idea. She knows about you and Lawrence now."

Bridget gaped at her. "She does? How did she find out?"

"I was forced to tell her," Fiona answered painfully. "You really should go. Your timing couldn't be worse! Miss Clara is hosting a masked ball tonight and she's frantic that something might go wrong!"

"But I've learned something terrible about Lawrence and I must tell someone immediately. He's not the person any of us thought he was!"

"Who is at the door?" Clara asked, walking toward Fiona and the open door. When she saw Bridget, her countenance fell.

"I'm sorry for coming so unexpectedly, Mrs. Collins, but there is something about Lawrence you must know!" she blurted.

Clara narrowed her eyes at Bridget. "I don't need you

to tell me anything about my husband. If you'll excuse me, I have a ball to attend to."

"But Clara, it is important!" Bridget persisted.

Clara felt her eyes filling with hot tears. "I don't wish to hear another word from you. It's time for you to leave, and please don't come back." Clara left for the stairs.

Fiona stared frightfully at Bridget. "I told you it was a bad time. Miss Clara has been in a sore mood since she got home yesterday. Mr. Collins was supposed to be back by now but has let Miss Clara down without so much as a phone call. It's probably why she does not want to hear anything about him."

Bridget hung her head in shame. "I didn't come to cause trouble, Fiona. Honest. I only wanted to warn her of the sort of man Lawrence really is."

Fiona groaned. "I think most of us are catching on. I'm sorry but I really must close the door now. Goodbye, sister."

Later that evening, before the start of the ball, Abigail was in her bedroom with Ethan and the baby, waiting for Serena to arrive. Abigail looked at the clock again. "She really should have been here by now. I wonder if she forgot."

Ethan looked up at Abigail from where he held the baby in the rocking chair. "Do we really have to go to this thing?" he asked sorrowfully. "I don't think I want to see all those people right now."

Abigail smiled compassionately at him. "If Serena is unable to come, you may be off the hook. I'm going to give her another few minutes before I go over to remind her."

Down the hallway, Clara sat pouting at her vanity table while Jane attended to her. "Mary was just called to a birth and won't be coming to the masquerade," she told Jane as she put on her jewelry. "I only hope nothing else goes wrong tonight."

It was as if Jane had read her mind. "Will Mr. Collins be arriving soon?"

Clara shrugged in irritation, feeling grateful for the mask that now hid her scowl. "Who knows if he will or not? I'm beginning to hope that he doesn't. And if Lawrence does come tonight, he might wish that he hadn't." Clara rose suddenly and checked her reflection before she walked away, leaving Jane bewildered in the room.

Still in her bedroom down the hallway, Abigail looked at the clock again. "Ethan, I'm just going next door to talk to Serena. I'll only be a few minutes. Will you be alright here with the baby?"

Ethan smiled as he continued to rock in the chair with the baby lying on his chest. "I'm sure we'll be just fine."

Abigail pulled on her coat and gloves before venturing outside into the cold night air. Serena could see her approaching from the window of the farmhouse. "Abigail is coming to the house," she cried. "Oh dear, I don't know what to tell her!"

Phillip was sitting on the floor with the children while they played a game. "You have to tell her something," he told his sister.

Serena panicked. "Just tell her I'm not feeling well today," she begged, then hurried to her room and closed the door.

"Serena, wait!" Phillip called after her. "You can't just run off!" Serena did not answer. The children looked up at their father when they heard Abigail knocking at the front door.

"Is Miss Abigail here?" Gabriella asked curiously.

Phillip sighed. "She's here. I just need to talk to her for a minute, alright? I'll come play again when I'm done."

"Alright," sighed Donnie.

Phillip rose from the floor and walked past the kitchen. He was not prepared for the wave of emotions that came over him when he saw Abigail on the other side of the door. "Good evening," he said, his voice cracking.

"Oh—" she stammered. "Good evening—um—I'm just here to remind Serena that she is caring for the baby tonight."

Phillip looked at the floor. "I'm sorry to tell you this, but my sister is unable to help at the house tonight."

"Oh?" Abigail responded, standing there awkwardly.

Phillip suddenly cringed. "I'm sorry, please come in. You shouldn't be standing out there in the cold."

Abigail smiled gratefully and stepped inside while Phillip closed the door behind her. Abigail could hear the children playing in the next room. "Is Serena alright?" she whispered.

"Uh—she's just—not feeling well," he stuttered.

Abigail became worried. "Oh dear. It's not the influenza, is it?"

"No, it's nothing like that," he said quickly, looking into her eyes. "But she's very sorry to not be able to come tonight."

"I see," Abigail replied.

"May I ask—" Phillip began nervously, "—if the little one is in good health?"

Abigail smiled. "Yes, he is very well."

"And—how are you? Are you doing well?"

"Yes," she whispered.

"Good," he nodded. "There's just one more thing I wondered. Have you chosen a name for him?"

"We are calling him Patrick…we will name him formally at the christening. It will be at Father Salvestro's home, before we move back to Philadelphia."

Phillip nodded again and swallowed painfully. "Of course. I wish you well with the christening…and with the move."

"Thank you," she answered. "I should go now. Please tell Serena that I hope she recovers quickly."

"I will," he promised. Phillip opened the door for Abigail and watched as she walked away into the night. He was startled by Serena's voice next to him.

"What was that all about?" she asked.

"What do you mean, 'what was that all about'?" he responded impatiently. "You were the one who disappeared and forced me to explain for you."

"I'm sorry about that, brother…but that's not what I meant. What's going on between you and Abigail?"

"Nothing is going on," he grumbled, not looking her in the eye. "I just don't like having to make up excuses for you."

"The way she looked at you…and the way you looked at her," Serena persisted. "It's as if you have been more than only neighbors."

Phillip could feel his face burning with embarrassment. "Let it go, Serena. You wouldn't understand."

Her mouth hung open at his response. "So there *is* something going on between you two!"

Phillip was quiet and began to walk back to where the children were playing. Serena grabbed his arm before he could leave. "What aren't you telling me?" she demanded. "Why are you so concerned about that baby? And why do you act funny whenever I mention him?"

Phillip clenched his jaw, still refusing to meet her gaze. "I never made you talk about Angelina when you didn't want to."

Serena let go of his arm and put her hand over her heart as she thought about his response. "Brother, what have you done? Tell me that I am misunderstanding—that the baby in Davenport House is not really your child!"

He glared at her. "It's not what you think." He walked away from the door and rejoined the children where they were playing on the floor. He sat down next to them as if he was ready to continue the game, but he held his head in his hands for a moment.

"Papa, are you alright?" asked Gabriella.

"I'm alright," he mumbled, doing his best to sound convincing. "Now, whose turn is it? Did you wait for me or did you play without me?"

Donnie handed him the dice. "We waited for you for a long long time," he answered.

Serena looked at the three of them and silently went back to her room, closing the door behind her.

At Davenport House, Abigail was just returning from her visit to the farmhouse. She went to her bedroom and smiled when she saw Ethan sitting there, contentedly holding the baby in his arms. "You are off the hook tonight," she giggled. "Serena cannot come after all. But poor Clara will be terribly disappointed that we are not down there."

Ethan shrugged, but seemed happy with the situation, and began to loosen his tie. "This is the best seat in the house as far as I'm concerned. It's getting noisy downstairs, anyway. I'd rather be up here with you and Patrick."

Abigail sat on the bed and removed her gloves to place

on the nightstand. Ethan suddenly jumped up from the rocking chair. "What was that?" he cried.

Abigail gasped, worried that Ethan would drop the baby in his frantic state. "I don't know what you mean, but why don't give Patrick to me," she said quickly. "It's time for him to eat."

Ethan held the baby to her with trembling hands. "It was a shooting sound. I don't know what it was!"

Abigail was confused, but more concerned that she took the little one before he fell from Ethan's grasp. "It's alright, I'll take him now."

Ethan crossed his arms over his chest and paced the room anxiously. Then he jumped again. "That's the sound! Did you hear it?"

"Oh—that—" she stammered. "It was just a champagne cork downstairs, I think."

Ethan covered his face with his hands. "I'm sorry, Abigail. I just can't do this. I can't be around all this racket." He hurried out of the room and Abigail looked out her window in time to see him heading out into the night in the direction of the stable.

Downstairs in the ballroom, a stir of excitement filled the air as ladies strutted through the room wearing their masks and matching evening gowns, holding the arms of gentlemen dressed in masks and tuxedos. Clara had finished cheerfully greeting the late-arriving guests, and she motioned to the orchestra to begin playing. Some guests began to dance while others stood near the elegantly set buffet tables.

At the same time, Fiona was rushing down the servants' stairs to her bedroom to change her apron. When she closed the door behind her, she began untying the apron strings of the one she had spilled on. A voice in the room made her jump with fright.

"Fiona?"

"Good grief, Bridget, you nearly scared me to death! What are you doing here?" she demanded.

"I had to come back so I could talk to Abigail," Bridget whimpered.

"After Miss Clara ordered you out of her house, you thought you would come back and stay in my room? I could be sacked for this!"

"No one saw me," Bridget promised. "I was very careful."

"That's not the point, Bridget!" she exclaimed in a panic. "Miss Clara said this party has to go perfectly. How am I supposed to make that happen while knowing you are hiding down here in my room?"

"I'll leave first thing tomorrow, I swear. There isn't another train to Philadelphia until the morning."

Fiona shook her head in disbelief. "You want to stay here overnight? Oh, I'm going to lose my job!"

"You won't lose your job," Bridget assured her. "No one will know. I bought this mask in town before I came here. I can sneak upstairs to Abigail's bedroom. I'm sure she won't tell anyone I've been here and I know how to be discreet in this house."

"I have to go back upstairs now," Fiona groaned as she tied on her new apron. "And I would hate to see you publicly ordered out of Miss Clara's house during the ball. For your sake, I hope you will change your mind about going upstairs."

When Fiona returned to the masquerade, the ballroom was in pandemonium. Guests were asking for their coats so they could leave. "Where have you been?" Clara demanded with wide eyes. "How could you order the maids to serve liquor at this party when half the guests are drys?"

Fiona stood gaping at Clara, unsure of how to answer. "It's what Mr. Collins insisted on, Miss Clara. I thought you agreed to it!"

A woman approached Clara just then with her nose high in the air. "I'm astonished at you, Mrs. Collins. I would never have attended your party if I knew the devil's drink was being served here. I thought you were a more sensible woman than that." She spun on her heel and led her husband away.

Clara looked at Fiona helplessly. "Remove every drop of alcohol from this room immediately! The guests have been quarreling ever since the champagne came out!"

Fiona could hear a man shouting from the crowd. "It's those Protestants who are keeping the rest of us from practicing our faith and having a good time! I say, drink up while we can!"

There were gasps and murmurs from the crowd. Fiona and Nora hurried around the room to collect every wine bottle and glass of champagne.

Abigail heard the commotion from downstairs and closed her bedroom door all the way, unsure of what was going on. She held Patrick in her arms and hummed to him while she looked out the window. "Why do you suppose the guests are leaving so soon?" she cooed in his ear. "I hope that Clara is not too upset." She heard the doorknob to her room turn and open just then. Abigail spun around to see who it was. "Bridget! What a surprise!"

"Forgive me for barging in like this, Abigail. I had to see you."

Abigail smiled and proudly held out her baby. "Come see my son. I had no idea you were in town."

Bridget gladly took the baby in her arms. "Oh, he is perfect."

Abigail lowered herself wearily into the rocking chair. "My arms were getting tired," she giggled. "How are you getting along at the manor house?"

Bridget looked at her solemnly. "Everything at the manor house is fine, but you should know is that I'm not supposed to be here. Clara ordered me out of the house this afternoon and told me not to come back."

Abigail raised her eyebrows. "That does not sound like Clara. Why would she react in such a drastic way?"

"I suppose it's because I came to tell her something terrible I learned about Lawrence."

Abigail cringed. "Yes, I suppose it was not the best timing for that."

"But it concerns you too," Bridget said mournfully.

"How could it concern me?"

Bridget explained everything that the new postman in Philadelphia had told her. Abigail covered her heart with her hands. "How awful!" She stood up to look out the window. "But it can't be. Lawrence and Clara were married before I received the news of Ethan."

Bridget shrugged uncertainly. "Perhaps there was a misunderstanding, and the note came later than he planned. Were you able to get an explanation from the war office?"

Painful tears stung behind her eyes when she responded. "I went to them for answers after Ethan returned home. They told me they could not understand who sent the note. There was no such captain as the one who signed the letter."

"Then surely it was Lawrence who arranged it. The evidence points to him," Bridget said angrily.

Abigail felt tears running down her cheeks. "How could one person…cause so much agony for so many? If I had never received that awful note—" She paused, wiping the tears from her face. "Things would be much different."

"I'm sorry to bring you this news, Abigail. I hope I did the right thing by telling you." Bridget carefully laid the sleeping baby into the cradle. "You could go to the police."

"I'm afraid of what it would do to Clara if I went to the police," Abigail responded. "Bridget…I'm more afraid of what Ethan might do if he heard about this. Please don't tell anyone else until I decide what I will do with the information."

Bridget nodded solemnly. "I won't tell. I should be leaving now before anyone sees me in the house. Goodbye, Abigail."

Downstairs in the house, Fiona and Nora were gathering coats for the masquerade guests who were leaving through the front door as quickly as they could exit.

Clara retreated alone to the gardens behind the house. She stood in the crisp night air, staring blankly past the courtyard, and almost didn't hear the soft voice from behind her.

"Mrs. Collins? Are you alright?"

She turned around to face Joe. "Didn't you notice that everything was a disaster? I wanted the masquerade to be widely remembered, but not like this! I don't know how I will show my face in town again."

Joe shrugged. "I thought it was a nice party."

Clara laughed. "Were we at the same party?"

He stifled a smile. "I'm sure we were. I noticed you

right away—mask and all. But anyway, it's freezing out here. Don't you want to go back inside?"

Clara shook her head. "It will only remind me of how dreadfully my party has failed. I'd rather stay out here and look out into the gardens where everything is rosy."

Joe removed his jacket and put it around Clara's shoulders. "If you insist, Mrs. Collins. It was good of you to host a party to cheer everyone, anyway. I'm sorry they were not as grateful to you as they should have been. I suppose people are getting tense about the new laws."

"Lawrence said that it will soon be illegal for us to even have wine in our own home…although I never know what to believe from him anymore…he promised he would be at the ball tonight. I suppose I've gotten so used to him breaking promises, that I would have been shocked if he actually did attend tonight."

Joe stood there awkwardly. "I'm sorry, Mrs. Collins. I figured he must have been quite a fellow for a fine lady like you to marry him."

Clara felt like laughing, but instead she looked at Joe thoughtfully. "Did you know that I used to be a housemaid here?"

"You, a housemaid?" he chuckled. "I don't believe it."

"It's true. I suppose there's a lot you don't know about me. It was only a few years ago that I began living the life of a lady. It's been an uphill battle to be accepted into society as I have always hoped to. Then Lawrence came along, and I thought he was my last chance at ever having a husband. I thought I might be taken more seriously when I was married, as the other married ladies are. But I'm afraid I was hasty in accepting Lawrence. In truth, I knew nothing about him or his life."

"I was sorry for not speaking up to you sooner. I guess it took me a while to work up the courage—" he cringed, "—after calling you an old spinster."

Clara laughed. "Yes, I remember like it was yesterday."

"Well, I sure hope things get better for you, Mrs. Collins. You deserve the best."

"I wish I'd never met Lawrence at all," she blurted. "I've done all I can to please him, but it has been miserable. In fact, as soon as he comes home again, I am going to talk to him about a divorce."

The following silence was suddenly broken by Nora clearing her throat behind them. "The orchestra has left, Mrs. Collins," she announced.

Clara felt sick to her stomach when she realized that Nora had been standing there, and Clara wondered how much of the conversation she might have heard. "Uh— very good—" she stuttered. "You may close up the ball-room now, and I'll be in shortly."

"Yes, Madam," Nora answered, and turned to go inside.

"I'd better be going," Joe told Clara. "Goodnight, Mrs. Collins." He left through the gardens while Clara remained in the courtyard, watching Joe walk back to his cottage.

Later that night, after the ballroom was closed and tidied, Fiona exited the servants' entrance to get some fresh air. Sam saw her sitting on the boulder alone and went to join her. "How did the party go?" he asked, seating himself on a tree stump across from her.

Fiona shook her head sadly. "This whole day was awful," she replied in despair.

"What happened?"

"Well, it began this afternoon when Miss Clara ordered my sister out of the house," she said, wiping a tear from her cheek. "Then a misunderstanding about the drinks at the party, which caused all the guests to fight and leave. I'm afraid Miss Clara blames me for everything. But it was Mr. Collins who gave instructions about the drinks."

"I'm sorry it went bad," he told her. "I still need to talk to Miss Clara about the deed. Maybe I should wait 'til she's not cross anymore about the party. But why did she say that to your sister?"

"Oh Sam, it's all a mess," Fiona said, covering her face with her hands. "I'm worried that I'll be sacked."

"You can't have done anything that bad," he said. "You wouldn't get sacked over a party gone wrong."

"Maybe not, but Bridget came back to the house after Miss Clara made her go. She is hiding in my room until she can take a train back to Philadelphia. If the other maids see her…or if Miss Clara sees her…I'm afraid of what might happen."

"I won't tell anyone," he promised.

"My family depends on me having this job," she continued.

"I understand," he said. "You won't lose your job. My sister says that no one could run a house as well as you."

Fiona managed a smile. "Thank you, Sam."

He stood up from the tree stump. "Are you going to be alright?"

"I hope so," she replied. "What about you?"

"I'll be alright…just as soon as I deal with Mr. Collins so I can get my title deed like I was supposed to."

Fiona nodded. "I should get back inside. Goodnight, Sam."

"Goodnight."

Late into the night, Sam was hurrying through the

servants' entrance, looking around to see if anyone was still awake. All was quiet and the lights were off. Sam quietly took the servants' stairs to the upper level of Davenport House. He went straight to Abigail's bedroom and entered without knocking.

"Abby…Abby, wake up." Sam gently shook her awake.

"Sam? What are you doing here?" she asked sleepily. Abigail sat up in bed and immediately checked on the baby, who was sleeping peacefully beside her. She shielded the baby's eyes while she switched on the bedside lamp. "What time is it?"

Sam did not answer. He looked at her with fear in his eyes. "I found Mr. Collins."

"Had he gone missing?" she questioned. "I did not realize. Where is he now?"

"In the field behind the stable. I tried to rouse him, but—he's dead, Abby."

Abigail drew a sharp breath. "Was Ethan with you?"

"No, he slept in his room the whole night. I didn't know what to do when I found Mr. Collins like that, so I came here to wake you. You know everyone in this house better than me. What do I do?"

"We must wake Clara and tell her there has been an accident. Mr. Collins will need to be carried inside so he may be laid out in the parlor. We will see to the burial when Clara is ready."

"Abby," Sam shook his head, lowering his voice to a whisper. "I don't think it was an accident."

Chapter 6

Clara stepped quickly through the servants' entrance and proceeded to remove her heels. The room was dark and the fires had not yet been lit. Clara held her shoes while she tip-toed past the servants' table in the kitchen. She stumbled over a chair in the dark and the lights were soon switched on. "Mrs. Collins?" Nora questioned in surprise. She stood in her nightgown holding a shawl around her shoulders and stared at Clara, who still wore her dress from the masked ball. "May I help with something?"

Clara stared back at her with wide eyes. "No, I just—I came down for a drink of water," she stammered.

Nora walked into the kitchen and poured a glass of water, setting it on a tray with a pitcher. "Is there anything else I can do for you, Mrs. Collins?"

"No, I'm just going back to bed," Clara whispered.

"Jane went to attend you in your room after the ball," Nora remarked. "But Mr. Collins told her that he did not know where you had gone."

"Nora, I'm very tired and only wish to go to bed. If

anyone needs me, tell them I am sleeping in the bedroom that used to be my mother's."

"Yes, Mrs. Collins. I can attend you, and help you out of your gown, if you wish."

Clara turned for the servants' stairs. "I will manage on my own. Goodnight."

"Goodnight, Mrs. Collins."

While Clara and Nora spoke in the servants' quarters, Sam and Abigail were leaving through the front door of the house to head for the stable. "Are you sure you want to try to wake Ethan? He's not the easiest person to get out of bed."

Abigail hugged the baby to her chest as she hurried along. "I think we must."

"You stay out here in the sitting room," Sam told her when they entered the apartment. "I'll go in and wake him."

Ethan snapped awake as soon as Sam pushed the door open. "What's happening? Is Abigail alright?" he asked quickly.

"She's in the sitting room," Sam replied. "Something bad happened, and we don't know what to do."

Ethan followed Sam to the sitting room where Abigail had settled in with the baby. "Lawrence is dead," she told him with wide eyes. "And we can't find Clara."

Ethan was stunned. "Has anyone called the police?"

Abigail shook her head. "Sam came to me in the house to tell me that he found a body outside. I went to Clara's bedroom to wake her, but she was not there. I became too frightened to stay in the house."

Ethan sat beside her and put his arm around her. "I can't believe this," he mumbled, and turned to Sam. "What happened?"

"I woke up when I heard a noise behind the stable. I put on my boots and went out there…and that's when I found him…he was all bloodied up like he got in a fight…"

"Did you check on Mary?" Ethan asked Abigail.

"She was called to a birth before the party last night and has not returned yet," she explained.

Ethan thought hard. "I'm going to go in the house to make sure the maids are alright and the police are called. You stay here with Sam until I get back."

Abigail nodded, the fear evident in her eyes. Ethan kissed her and the baby, then went to remove a rifle from the gun cabinet. "I want to be prepared in case I run into whoever did this," he said.

Ethan entered the house through the servants' door and went straight to the door of the housekeeper's room.

Fiona was startled awake by his knock at her door. She turned to Bridget who was sleeping beside her. "Bridget," she whispered frantically, shaking her awake. "Someone is knocking at my door."

Bridget opened her eyes and nodded, leaving the bed to hide behind the room divider. Fiona held a shawl over her shoulders and nervously opened the door, afraid that Clara had found out about Bridget being there. Fiona was stunned when she opened the door to see Ethan standing there with the rifle. Her eyes were wide with alarm.

"I don't want to frighten you," he said. "But there's been a death on the estate. I need you to make sure the staff is alright."

Fiona nodded solemnly and proceeded to wake the maids and cook. They all gathered in the servants' lobby while Ethan addressed them. "I'm afraid that Mr. Collins has been found dead outside," he began. The maids gasped and covered their faces with their hands. "We're worried about Clara. She was not found in her room."

"Mrs. Collins is sleeping in her mother's old room tonight," Nora spoke up.

"Then we need to wake her and tell her what's happened," Ethan responded. "I'm going back outside to have a look around. Fiona, call the police. You should also have someone get the parlor ready for when we bring the body inside."

"Yes, Mr. Ethan," she nodded.

"I'll explain to Mrs. Collins," Nora said, then disappeared up the servants' stairs.

At the stable apartment, Abigail turned worriedly to Sam. "I hope the Valentis are alright. Maybe you should check on them since Lawrence was found so near their property."

"I'll check on them after Ethan gets back," Sam told her.

Ethan came through the door just then. "Clara is at the house," he said. "The maids told me she slept in her mother's room last night."

Abigail breathed in relief. "Thank God. I was worried for her when I saw her bed empty."

Ethan continued solemnly as he returned the rifle to the gun cabinet. "I—I had a look at Mr. Collins. I didn't see anyone else around, but the police will be on their way soon. Maybe we shouldn't move the body until they get here."

Sam nodded and rose from his seat. "I'm going to check on our neighbors. Maybe they saw or heard something at the farmhouse."

After Sam left the apartment, Abigail began crying. "Clara will be distressed to hear the news. But if I go to comfort her now, I must only pretend that I am sorry Lawrence is dead. What if it is all my fault?"

Ethan was bewildered. "How could any of this be your fault?"

"I wished him dead last night," she confessed. "I never dreamed it would actually happen."

Ethan felt his heart sink. "Has he done something to you? Something you never told me?"

"I only learned about it last night," she said mournfully. "He has done something dreadful…to the both of us."

"You and the baby?" Ethan asked in horror.

"No, to you and me. Bridget came to the house last night to inform me—the letter that came from the war office about your death—it was Lawrence who arranged for it to be sent! It was with the intent to trick me into being with him!"

Ethan's confused expression turned to rage. "If I knew of this last night…" he trailed off.

"It was a detestable plan," she continued. "I was going to speak with Clara about it today, but there is no reason to now. I'm only glad he is dead and can do no more damage."

The room was silent when Sam emerged through the door again. "I talked to Phillip. The family is good. They didn't see or hear anyone last night."

"Thank you, Sam," Abigail said to him. "I suppose we must wait for the police to arrive and tell us what should be done next." Sam and Ethan nodded in agreement, and they sat quietly in the apartment, waiting for the police.

At Davenport House, Clara was opening her eyes sleepily. "What is it, Nora?"

"The police are on their way," she answered.

"What do you mean?" Clara asked groggily. "Why are the police coming?"

"Because of Mr. Collins, Madam."

Clara sat up quickly. "What are you saying?"

"The police are coming to investigate who might have done such a thing…to cause his death…" She gingerly lifted Clara's gown from the chair and hung it up in the wardrobe.

Clara was aghast. "What happened?"

"It's what the police will want to know. Should I tell them that you have been sleeping in your mother's room all night?"

Clara went pale and began to sweat. "Nora, I'm in shock. Are you telling me that my husband is dead?"

"Yes, Madam."

Fiona entered the room just then. "The police chief has arrived, Mrs. Collins."

Clara looked between Nora and Fiona with wide eyes. "Please tell the chief that I am distressed and unable to come downstairs."

"Yes, Madam," Fiona answered, and walked away. Chief Reynolds arrived in Clara's doorway shortly afterward.

"I am sorry for your loss, Mrs. Collins," he said, holding his hat and bowing his head.

"I have only just learned of my husband's passing, Sir. I'm still in shock," Clara replied.

"Of course," he said. "I'm afraid that I must open an investigation into your husband's death. It means that I will question your staff today, but we'll be sure to stay out of your way."

Clara nodded with wide eyes.

"I don't wish to bother you during your time of grief,

but there is something I must ask before I go downstairs," the chief resumed.

"Yes?" Clara squeaked.

"Do you know who may have done this? Did your husband have enemies who may have wanted to injure him?"

Clara felt her heart racing in her chest. "I'm afraid I don't know the answer to that, Sir."

Chief Reynolds nodded and turned to Nora. "Miss, please follow me downstairs where I will ask you some questions."

"Yes, Sir," Nora answered, but she gave Clara a reassuring look before she left the room.

Downstairs in the parlor, Sam and Ethan laid the body of Mr. Collins on the table. Ethan covered the face with a linen and gave Sam a look. "I suppose we should tell Clara that we've brought him in."

Ethan went upstairs to Clara's room, where Abigail was with her. "We laid him out downstairs," Ethan said quietly. "If you want to see him—"

"Is the police chief still here?" Clara interrupted.

"No, he already left," Ethan sighed.

"Then I want you to call the undertaker to come for Lawrence right away," she said.

Ethan nodded and left the room.

"Are you certain you don't want to look upon him or say goodbye for the last time?" questioned Abigail gently.

Clara shook her head. "It was no great secret that Lawrence and I were not getting along. I found out that he lied to me about his mother. I don't think I could stand the sight of him right now, alive or dead."

"I understand," she replied, understanding more than Clara might realize. "Should I have the maids bring you breakfast?"

"I'm not hungry," Clara replied. "I think I just wish to be left alone for awhile." Abigail kissed her on the forehead then stood up to leave the room. Before she was out of the doorway, Clara added quickly, "Oh Abigail, I have changed my mind. I do want breakfast—only, could you be sure that Nora brings it up to me?"

"I will see to it," Abigail promised, then left the room.

Downstairs in the servants' quarters, Fiona went to her bedroom and closed the door behind her. "Bridget," she whispered.

Bridget walked out into view. "What's happening out there?"

"The undertaker has arrived and is taking Mr. Collins," Fiona said with wide eyes. "The police are gone now and everyone is upstairs paying their respects. You should leave through the servants' door now when no one will see you."

Bridget stared at Fiona in horror. "Lawrence is dead?"

"Yes, but we don't have time to talk about it now!"

Bridget nodded and gathered her things. "Did the police say who did it?"

"I don't think they know," Fiona said, her voice filled with anxiety. "Hurry, sister. I'm afraid that someone will see you." Bridget followed her to the servants' door where Fiona stood watch as she hurried away from the house.

Upstairs in Clara's bedroom, Nora entered the doorway. "I have your breakfast, Madam," she said, bringing the tray toward the bed.

"Leave it on the tea table for now," Clara said.

"Yes, Madam." Nora set the tray down and turned toward Clara. "Is there anything else you wish me to bring you?"

Clara hesitated. "I wish to speak to you a moment. Close the door please."

Nora closed the door and looked at Clara expectantly.

"Did you say anything to the police…about me?" she asked nervously.

"I told him you wished to sleep in your mother's bed-room last night, and that I attended you after the ball."

"I see," Clara said, looking down at the bed. "And was that—all you said about me?"

"It was, Madam," Nora replied. "I thought it best to not speak of my running into you in the kitchen just hours ago—when you had come in from outside."

Clara did not look her in the eye. "Then I may count on your discretion?"

"I used to be housekeeper in a grand house like this, Mrs. Collins. There are always secrets to be kept and maids who must show discretion."

"The conversation I had last night in the courtyard… may I rely on you to be discrete about that as well?"

Nora looked at her smugly. "I think I might be persuaded."

Clara raised her eyebrows. "What do you mean?"

"You're asking a lot of me, Mrs. Collins—much more than a Mistress usually asks of a mere housemaid."

Clara had a sinking feeling and regretted that she asked Nora to bring the breakfast. "What do you want?" she asked in a low voice.

"I only would like a position in the house respective to the secrets I keep for its Mistress," Nora replied.

Clara sighed. "Very well. I'll tell Fiona that you may attend me now instead of Jane. We will call you senior housemaid."

Nora frowned at her. "I am capable of much more than that, Mrs. Collins."

"I don't understand what position you want, then," Clara said impatiently.

"I think I could manage the house in a way that pleases you," Nora replied.

Clara scoffed. "How would I explain such a transition to Fiona, or the others?"

Nora shrugged slightly. "Fiona was supposed to ensure the masquerade ran perfectly, but after the failure that it was…perhaps she should not be surprised if you wanted someone else to run things."

Clara was quiet while she contemplated the changes that Nora was asking for.

Outside the house, Sam observed that Fiona was standing near the servants' door, looking into the distance. "Are you alright?" he asked.

Fiona jumped when she heard his voice. "No, I'm not alright," she said, but would not look him in the eye. "I barely slept. I've been afraid since Mr. Collins was found."

Sam did not seem bothered. "Well, he only got what he had coming to him. If you knew what he did to my sister, you would know how well he deserved it."

Fiona was aghast. "Sam—what have you done?"

"Me? I haven't done nothing!" he cried defensively.

"Oh—then it wasn't you—who—?" Fiona stammered.

The hurt was evident in his eyes. "You think I had something to do with this?"

"I—I'm sorry—it's just that you were so mad after Mr. Collins tricked you with that contract! You said you would make him pay, and I was afraid when I heard something happened to him!"

"Mr. Collins was a bad man, but it wasn't me who did that to him," he said emotionally, turning his face away from her. "If you want to know what really happened to him last night, then maybe you should ask your sister!"

Sam hurried away before Fiona could see how much her comment had upset him.

Fiona remained at the servants' entrance, stunned at the suggestion that Sam had made before he left. She wondered what Bridget could have known about any of it, when Nora walked out the servants' door to speak to her. "The Mistress wishes to have a word with you," she sneered, looking Fiona up and down. "She's in her room."

Fiona turned to look at her. "Why are you staring at me like that?" she demanded.

Nora smiled wickedly. "You'll find out soon enough."

Fiona stumbled into the house, taking each heavy step up the servants' stairs, while a feeling of dread came over her. She became convinced that Clara learned about her hiding Bridget in the house. When Fiona entered Clara's bedroom, it was all she could do to remain upright. "You wished to see me, Madam?"

Clara swallowed the lump in her throat. "What I have to say is very difficult for me, after how well you have served this house in the past years…"

Fiona hung her head in shame. "Am I being fired?"

Clara was bewildered that Fiona seemed to expect punishment at all, but she continued anyway. "I don't wish for you to leave altogether, Fiona," she said quietly. "I hope that you'll stay on as a housemaid."

Fiona looked up at her. "You are gracious to me, Miss Clara."

"In the meantime, I'm going to ask Nora to take over as housekeeper…"

Fiona felt sick to her stomach, but nodded anyway. She bowed her head and left the room, wiping the tears from her eyes as she descended the servants' stairs. When she got to her room, she saw that Nora was in there sitting on the bed. "What are you doing in here?"

Nora snickered. "I'm just looking at my new room. Now Fiona, I am going into town to get a suitable dress for my new position. It will give you enough time to take your things out of here and get settled into the room that used to be mine. You can move my things in when you're through moving out. There's a housemaid uniform waiting for you in the laundry room."

"Alright," Fiona said as calmly as she could. "I will get everything moved while you are gone."

"See that you do," Nora said smugly before she pulled on her coat and left the house.

Chapter 7

Mary strained to hold back tears from the situation unfolding before her, but it was no use. She cast a panicked glance toward David, the brother of the woman who Mary was attending. "Can I do something to help her, Mrs. Hamilton?" he asked.

"Just keep holding the baby…and keep praying," she whispered, her voice shaking. David nodded solemnly.

Mary turned to the woman who had just delivered. "I am going to put in more stitches," she told her.

The woman gazed fixedly past Mary. "It'll be alright, Mrs. Hamilton. My husband is here. He'll take me to Heaven."

Mary felt the hair on her neck stand up. She knew that the woman's husband died in the War, and the presence Mary felt over her shoulder just then gave her goosebumps all over. Her heart raced when she observed the woman's bleeding become worse, despite all of Mary's efforts. "Stay with us, Mildred," she pleaded. David paced the room beside her. Mary's hands shook as she tried to thread the needle again.

David then spoke up mournfully. "I don't think you'll need to do that anymore, Mrs. Hamilton."

When Mary looked up, she saw that Mildred lay there with eyes still open, but there was no life behind them. She checked for a heartbeat or any sign of life. "I am sorry," she finally said to David, bowing her head.

"You did what you could," he responded, taking the baby with him to the sitting area.

Mary trembled as she cleaned the room and packed her kit. She laid a quilt over Mildred and gently closed her eyelids.

"I'm terribly sorry, David," she said again when she saw him in the sitting area of the house.

David looked sorrowfully at the baby in his arms. "Mrs. Hamilton, I can't take care of this little one. I just signed on with the railroad and they expect me to start tomorrow. I s'pose I'll send word for the undertaker first thing in the morning."

Mary nodded sadly. "Is there a friend or relative who could take the child?"

David shook his head. "I'm 'fraid not."

Mary seated herself in a chair while she tried to think. "I could take the baby to the parish in Yorktown, if you permit me. The minister will find a home for him."

David held the baby out to Mary. "Thank you, Mrs. Hamilton. I think I ought to get to sleep before I start work tomorrow." He wiped a tear from his eye and left Mary in the sitting area.

Mary looked helplessly at the baby in her arms. "I'm sorry," she whispered. "We'll find you a home as soon a possible." She bundled the baby warmly and took him out through the cold night air to her car, where she set up a bed for the baby to lie in. Mary drove to the parish in Yorktown, hoping that the minister's family might still be awake. She was encouraged to see that a light was showing through the windows.

She parked the car in the driveway and walked up to the door with the baby in her arms. She raised her hand to knock but stopped herself when she noticed the red ribbon hanging from the door. "Oh no," she whispered. Mary returned to the car with the baby and set up a place for him again. She cried over the steering wheel while she tried to think of another plan. As she was driving away, she remembered a stop she could make on her way home to Davenport House.

Father Salvestro was awake when the knock came at his door. He opened it to see Mary holding the baby. "Do you need help, Miss?"

"Good evening, Sir—um—Father—" she said awkwardly. "I—this little one is an orphan and I don't know what to do with him."

He smiled kindly and took the baby in his arms. He noticed that Mary was pale and trembling as she stood in the doorway. "Come in, Miss. When did you last eat?"

Mary felt her knees going weak as the priest helped her to the sofa. "I am sorry to bother you at this time of night," she was saying.

"It's no trouble," he replied, setting the kettle on the stove to boil. "You just rest a moment before you return on your way."

"Thank you," she said. She held her head in her hands and began to sob. The priest found a basket to lay the baby in and brought Mary a tray of tea and bread. "Have we met before, Miss?"

Mary nodded as she dried her face. "It was only once before. Abigail is my sister-in-law. You came to our house once."

"Ah yes," the priest remembered kindly. "Then you are my neighbor in the grand house."

"My name is Mary Hamilton. My husband runs the clinic in Yorktown."

"I've heard great things about the both of you, Mrs. Hamilton. You are the county midwife."

Mary nodded again. "I attended the birth of this child's mother. The mother has now passed on. I don't know what I did wrong. I did everything just as I usually do, but..." Tears were falling down her face again.

"It may have been her time," he replied gently.

"I first took the child to the parish in town, but the family is suffering from influenza. I hoped that you might know of someone who could care for the baby."

"We have nurses at the convent," he replied. "The child will be well looked after."

Mary breathed in relief. She drank the tea and ate the bread gratefully. "Thank you, Father. I should be getting home now." She reached into her purse and handed him several coins. "This is for your train fare to the convent... and for the child's wellbeing."

The priest nodded humbly, accepting the coins and showing Mary to the door. "Bless you, Mrs. Hamilton. Goodnight."

The next morning at Davenport House, Abigail visited Clara's bedroom at breakfast time. "How are you feeling today, Clara?"

"Awful," she answered. "I still can't believe any of this is happening. I can't imagine who could have done such a thing to Lawrence, but the police say they are looking into it."

Fiona walked into the room just then with Clara's breakfast tray. "Breakfast for you, Mrs. Collins," she said quietly. She did not look Abigail in the eye and left quickly after she set the tray on the table.

Abigail looked at Clara in confusion. "I wonder why Fiona is wearing a maid's uniform today."

"Oh—um—I suppose I forgot to tell you," Clara stammered. "Fiona is working as a maid again. I am trying out Nora as our housekeeper."

Abigail was shocked, but she could tell that Clara did not want to speak further about it. Abigail changed the subject. "I saw Mary's car in the driveway this morning. She must have returned from the birth late last night."

"She really is working herself too hard," Clara remarked. "I worry for the baby if she keeps up this pace."

"I worry too," sighed Abigail. "But I just realized that she hasn't been home since the night of the ball. I will go and explain to her that the house is now in mourning for Lawrence."

Clara stared blankly in front of her and did not respond. Abigail brought the breakfast tray to the bed for her. "Have some breakfast so you may keep your strength," Abigail said, kissing Clara on the cheek.

"Thank you, dear. Don't worry about me for now. You should check on Mary and make sure she eats her breakfast this morning."

Abigail knocked softly on Mary's bedroom door, which was ajar. "Come in," Mary answered weakly.

She walked into the dark room and asked, "Should I open the curtains?"

"No. I am very tired."

"Oh, I'm sorry," Abigail replied. "I don't wish to bother you, Mary, but there is something that you should know. Something dreadful happened while you were gone."

Mary sat up in alarm. "Is it William? I've been so worried for him lately, and I cannot reach him at the clinic!"

"No, it is not about William," Abigail said quickly. Mary lay back down and Abigail continued. "It is about Lawrence. He has passed away."

Mary turned on the lamp on the nightstand, her mouth hanging open in astonishment. "What happened? Oh no, Clara must be devastated at being widowed so young."

"It is worse than that, Mary," she replied, cringing. "The police think someone may have killed him here on the estate."

"My word!" Mary cried in a whisper. "Who do they think has done it?"

Abigail looked at her helplessly. "The police are investigating, and have already questioned the servants. Today they may return to question us as well. But they have not said whether they suspect anyone."

"I can't believe this," Mary said. "Was it the night of the ball?"

"It was. But Lawrence was never at the ball, which I am told ended badly."

"I only hope that Clara will recover," Mary sighed. "It must be terrible for her to be questioned at a time like this."

Abigail looked at her carefully. "Mary, you have been crying. What's wrong?"

Mary looked away from her as tears filled her eyes again. "I—I am very tired—and I worry for William."

Fiona walked in with a breakfast tray just then and

quickly set it on the tea table before she left. Mary turned to Abigail. "Was that Fiona? Why is she dressed like that?"

Abigail sighed heavily. "Apparently, Clara has given Nora the position of housekeeper. Fiona is now just a maid."

"Why on earth would Clara switch them? I can't imagine Fiona doing anything to deserve such treatment."

"I don't understand it either. Things have been tense and strange in the house since Lawrence was found."

The sound of a crying baby interrupted them both as Ethan peered into the doorway, holding the little one in his arms. "I'm sorry, ladies," he apologized. "He must be ready to eat."

"I'll be in my room in just a moment," Abigail told him. Ethan left the doorway and Abigail brought the breakfast tray to Mary's bed. "I'm more concerned that you're the one not getting enough to eat. You are working too hard, especially in your condition."

"I have to," Mary replied wearily. "There is no one else to do it! Anyway, I am too tired to eat. I only want to sleep."

"Alright, Mary," she said with a frown. "I'll leave the tray here for when you change your mind." Mary nodded and pulled the quilt up around her, settling in for sleep.

Later that morning when Abigail had finished nursing the baby, she went to the library to telephone the clinic. "Good morning," she said to the nurse who answered. "My name is Abigail Smith and I wish to speak with Dr. Hamilton."

The nurse was hesitant. "I'm sorry, Miss Smith. Dr. Hamilton is not available at this time. You might try back in a week or so."

"A week or so?" Abigail questioned. "Oh, I should have

mentioned that I am not calling as a patient, but on behalf of Dr. Hamilton's wife, Mary Hamilton."

The nurse was quiet for a moment. "Perhaps I can take a message for Dr. Hamilton."

"Yes, please tell William that it is urgent he call the house as soon as possible," Abigail told her.

"I will relay the message, Miss Smith. Goodbye."

Downstairs in the servants' quarters, Nora sent Fiona to help the cook in the kitchen. Mrs. Malone eyed Fiona curiously. "What's going on? Why are you lettin' Nora pretend to be housekeeper?"

Fiona looked down at the butcher block table as she cleared away the potato peels. "Nora is not pretending. Miss Clara has decided that she should be housekeeper from now on."

Mrs. Malone was skeptical. "It doesn't make a lick of sense. Nothing around this house makes any sense. Nora struts around here all high and mighty, but it doesn't mean she is fit for the job. And why would you tolerate being a maid here again, anyway? You could be housekeeper at another grand house, surely."

Fiona was hesitant. "I don't know that Miss Clara will give me a good reference for it. I'm being disciplined."

"Oh," Mrs. Malone mumbled. "Still…it doesn't seem right…"

Nora entered the kitchen just then, looking irritated. "If you two put as much effort into your work as you did discussing matters that are not your concern, the luncheon would be ready by now." Mrs. Malone laughed defiantly and Nora glared at her. "Perhaps you don't need the help after all, Mrs. Malone. Fiona, you can clean the washrooms of the upstairs bedrooms."

"I already did this morning," Fiona said quietly.

"Then do it again!" Nora demanded before she turned on her heel to leave the kitchen.

Fiona looked helplessly at Mrs. Malone, who was shaking her head in annoyance. "She won't be housekeeper for long acting like that." Fiona did not reply, but gathered the cleaning supplies and headed up the servants' stairs.

At the Valentis' farmhouse, Serena was heading to the kitchen after putting Donnie and Gabriella down for their afternoon nap. She noticed that Phillip was just closing the front door after speaking to someone. "Who was at the door?" she asked.

Phillip went to the sitting area and lowered himself onto the sofa. "The police were asking if we saw anyone suspicious wandering around that night."

Serena looked at Phillip expectantly. "Well? What did you tell them?"

He shrugged. "I said we had already gone to sleep by then and didn't see anything."

Serena's eyes were wide with fright. "You didn't tell the police about Lawrence being Angelina's father did you?"

"Of course I didn't tell them. The last thing we need is them thinking you are connected to this whole mess. Have you heard back from that investigator?"

"No," she mumbled, looking away from him.

Phillip lowered his voice. "Look, I know what I said that night when you told me about Lawrence—but it wasn't me who did this to him. You believe me, don't you?"

"I believe you, brother," she said, but she would not look him in the eye.

"You've been acting like you don't trust me anymore. I wouldn't lie about something like this."

"Why won't you tell me what happened with you and Abigail?" she questioned him.

Phillip groaned. "I think everyone is just trying to forget the whole thing, and I suppose I should too."

"Donnie told me that Abigail used to be his mother, and that he wishes she could live here again. I told Donnie that he must be mistaken, and explained that she only stayed here to care for them while I was away. But Gabriella confirmed that Abigail was indeed their mother."

Phillip was reluctant to answer and his throat tightened in pain. "Abigail lived with us for a short time. It was before she learned that her husband was coming home. She had a death note about him from the war office long before that, and we all believed she was a widow. She came here to be the children's mother…and to be my wife. She left us the moment she heard her husband was still alive."

Serena was quiet as the words sunk in. "And the baby? You believe him to be yours?"

Phillip stared blankly at the fireplace. "The baby can never be mine. The truth is, I wouldn't be here at all if it weren't for Ethan Smith. We were close like brothers during the War…I asked him to be a father to my children if I didn't make it back. So you see, I won't claim his only son. No, I'll just count my blessings that I'm still here and have Gabriella and Donnie. It's not going to do good for anyone to think beyond that."

Serena felt pained to look upon his anguished face. She rose from her seat to leave the room, but first spoke to him solemnly, "I'm sorry for the loss you have endured over the years, brother. You are a true and honest man and surely deserve better. Forgive me for not understanding…I won't ask you to speak of it again." She quietly went to her room while Phillip remained where he was, watching the flames in the fireplace.

Later that evening at Davenport House, Nora was announcing to Abigail that she had a telephone call. Abigail hurried to the library to answer it. "Hello?"

A hoarse voice spoke from the other end. "Abigail, is Mary alright?"

"Mary is—alright—" she stammered. "Am I speaking with William?"

"Yes, it's me," he answered.

"Oh. You don't sound like yourself."

"The nurse said that you called urgently about Mary…"

"Oh, yes I do need to speak with you. Mary is terribly overworked, you see. She is not taking care of herself. She seems depressed and I can't persuade her to eat. I wondered if you or someone from the Red Cross could assist with the births so that Mary can have the rest she needs."

William was quiet for so long that Abigail worried the connection had been lost. He finally spoke. "I don't want Mary to know this, but I've been ill these past weeks. I'm in quarantine now."

Abigail felt her heart sink. "Oh, William!" she replied sorrowfully.

"I've done all I can think of to fight it, but the fever is constant. I don't want to burden Mary with the thought of me being ill at a time like this."

"Of course," Abigail whispered.

"I'll do what I can to find her help with the births," he continued. "But Abigail, promise me you will care for Mary and make her eat!"

"I promise," she told him. "And promise me you will take care of yourself. We miss you desperately at the house."

"I'll do my best," he answered. "Goodbye."

Late that night, down the road from Davenport House, Father Salvestro was returning home from the train station. He noticed Serena waiting outside the door of his house. "Come inside the house, child. It is too cold to stand out here."

"Thank you, Father," she answered, following him through the front door.

The priest knelt down in front of the fireplace to begin adding logs to the embers. "How have you been, child? I've not seen you in a while."

Serena found a chair and sat down. "I hoped that I could give confession tonight, for it might be too late if I wait any longer."

The priest nodded and seated himself at the tea table. "I welcome you to give confession tonight, if you wish."

Serena took a deep breath and closed her eyes before she began. "Bless me, Father, for I have sinned. It has been four years since my last confession, and these are my sins…"

"Go on, child."

Serena continued sorrowfully. "I have broken the fifth commandment."

"The fifth commandment?" the priest repeated.

"Yes…I have killed. I killed my child's father."

CHAPTER 8

William struggled to keep his eyes open as he drove the winding road into the mountains. He parked the car to the side of the dirt road and groaned in pain as he climbed out. The aches and chills overwhelmed his body, but he was determined to endure the hike up the hill into the trees. When he could see a log cabin in the distance, he cleared his throat and spoke as strongly as his voice would allow. "Miss Jenkins!"

Greta Jenkins could not hear him from inside the cabin, but her dog sat whimpering at the front door. "You think someone is out there?" she asked. She opened the door while her dog went running to William, who had fallen to the ground and lay shivering. "Dr. Hamilton?" she asked. "You don't look so good."

His teeth chattered as he spoke. "My wife needs help."

"Your wife? Looks like you're the one who needs help." She took his arm and helped him to his feet, proving herself to be much stronger than she looked. "Come inside the house," she said. It was the last thing that William heard before he blacked out.

When he opened his eyes again, he found himself on a log bed near a crackling fire. He fought to remember where he was or how he got there. Greta stepped toward him and said, "Drink this, quickly."

He sat up in bed as best he could and took the tall mug from her. As he drank the foul smelling liquid, he had to repress the urge to spit it out. His stomach turned when it hit and he started to sweat heavily.

Greta leaned over William and searched his face as he shivered and sweated. "You'll be alright," she finally said. "So long as you can keep that tea down."

William grimaced as his stomach turned into knots, but it was not long before he felt himself falling back into a deep sleep.

At Davenport House, Abigail was in her room feeding the baby when Sam appeared in her doorway. "Hello, Sam. What is it?"

Sam walked in and sat at the tea table. "How are you… after everything?"

Abigail forced a smile. "I'm alright, I suppose. But the house seems to be falling apart around me. At least I got Mary to eat her dinner last night."

Sam nodded and was about to speak, but Fiona entered the room just then with a mop and bucket. She froze when she observed that Sam was in the room, and she quickly looked away. "I'm sorry, Miss Abigail. I have just come to clean the washroom. I'll return later."

Abigail was confused. "You've already cleaned the washroom today. It's not necessary to clean it again."

Fiona's chin trembled and she looked at the floor. "It's Nora's orders that the washrooms be cleaned twice a day now."

Abigail felt impatient. "That's silly, Fiona. Please attend to your other work. My washroom is fine for the day."

"Yes, Miss Abigail," Fiona said, then left the room.

Abigail looked at Sam, who had been staring at Fiona the whole time. Abigail's words snapped him out of his daze. "Don't ask me why, but Clara has decided that Nora should be the housekeeper."

"I know…it's what I came to talk to you about," he muttered back.

"It is? Why?"

Sam felt his jaw clench with emotion. "It ain't right the way they're treating Fiona. She deserves to be housekeeper the same as she was before. Nora is making extra work for her just to be a pain in the neck. I've seen Nora make a mess just to watch her clean it up!"

Abigail frowned. "I was afraid of how this was going over downstairs. How miserable it must be for Fiona."

"I hoped you could put a stop to it and make Fiona the housekeeper again."

"But Sam, this isn't my house. Clara decides matters among the staff here."

"Well, can't you talk to her about it?"

"It isn't my place. Besides, it would be a terrible time to bother her about such a thing. Poor Clara must plan her own husband's funeral."

Sam looked down in disappointment. "I suppose. But it still ain't right what they're doing to Fiona."

Abigail looked at him carefully. "Did you really come in here to talk about Fiona?"

Sam felt his cheeks turning red. "She's a nice girl and she deserves better. I hoped that you could help her… that's all."

Abigail smiled at him knowingly. "I'll see what I can do. But I can't make any promises."

"Thanks, Abby," he said, rising from his seat. "I should be getting back to work now."

"Alright, Sam. Have a good day." After Sam left the room, Abigail laid the baby in the wooden cradle and went to look out her window. She heard Ethan's voice behind her.

"Is Patrick asleep already?" he asked.

"He was just awake, but it seldom lasts long," she answered, stifling a yawn. "I hoped that Serena would be helping me daily by now. I'm afraid I need her now more than ever since I'm looking after Mary too."

"Is Mary alright?"

Abigail shook her head. "She seems terribly upset about something, but I don't know what it is."

"Is it since you told her about the death that happened here?"

"No," she sighed. "Mary was upset even before that. I only hope that William may return home soon, and things can go back to normal."

"I hardly remember what normal is like," Ethan mumbled. "Why don't you find out what's going on with Serena at least? I'll stay here with Patrick."

Abigail smiled in relief and kissed Ethan's cheek. "I hope I can persuade her to help me tonight. Then I might sleep for a little while." She pulled on her coat and walked next door to the Valentis' farmhouse.

Phillip answered the door, raising his eyebrows in surprise. "Hello," he greeted.

"Good afternoon," she replied shyly. "Um—I have come to speak with Serena. I hope she is feeling better now."

Phillip looked sadly into her eyes. "Serena is resting in her room. Why don't you come in and have a seat? There's something you should know."

"Oh? Um—yes, I will come in for a moment."

They sat across from each other in the kitchen and Phillip began to explain. "I'm aware that you made an arrangement with my sister…that you lent her money and expect her to pay you back by caring for—for your baby."

"Yes…has Serena changed her mind?"

Phillip nodded. "I'll make sure you get your hundred dollars back, but it might take me awhile. I'm sorry about all this."

Abigail looked at him worriedly. "Tell me the truth, Phillip. Have I done something to offend Serena? I don't understand why she will not come back."

Phillip groaned within himself, knowing that hearing the truth was the only way Abigail would not blame herself. He lowered his voice. "It's not you, Abigail. I don't suppose my sister ever told you about the father of her baby."

"She never said a word," Abigail whispered.

"My sister hadn't seen Angelina's father since she told him she was with child. But the night Serena returned from Pittsburgh and met with you, she came back in a fright after seeing—him—at Davenport House."

"Angelina's father was at the house?" she asked incredulously. "What was he doing there?"

"He lived there…as Clara's husband."

Abigail stared at him with wide eyes. When she found her voice, she whispered frantically, "How long have you known about this?"

"She told me the night of the masquerade when she was supposed to help with the baby. I was furious with

Lawrence when Serena told me…but I didn't have anything to do with what happened to him that night."

Abigail put her hand over her heart. "No, of course not. This is all so shocking. Does Clara know about Angelina?"

"Not unless Lawrence told her, which Serena and I both doubt. He was inclined to lie about things."

"Yes, I know," Abigail said bitterly. "Things are just awful at the house right now while the investigation is ongoing. I'm worried for Clara because the police are coming to question her tomorrow. We will have no peace at the house until we understand what happened that night."

Serena emerged from her room just then, appearing as if she had heard their conversation. "The police won't bother Clara tomorrow," she said, bowing her head in shame. "I'm going to turn myself in. It was me who killed him."

Phillip and Abigail gaped at Serena in horror. She looked at them sorrowfully. "I'm sorry I caused so much trouble. I never meant to hurt everyone. And I'm sorry about your hundred dollars, Abigail."

"I am not worried about the money," Abigail said breathlessly. "I am worried for you! What about Angelina?"

Serena shrugged. "I can't change what has already happened. I only hope that if the investigator brings my daughter home, my brother might take care of her."

Phillip stared at her in disbelief. "I don't understand. Surely, you did not do this thing."

"I didn't know that I killed him until later when they told us he was dead. I thought I only hurt him. He was on his way here to hurt me."

"He came here?" Phillip questioned angrily.

"I saw him through my window. He was approaching the farmhouse, but one of the maids from the house stopped him. He was going to hurt her and I was afraid… so I took a shovel from the garden and hit him from behind. When he fell down, I ran back into the house and locked the door."

"Serena, why didn't you wake me?" Phillip cried emotionally. "I would have helped you bury him where no one could find him!"

"I swear I never knew that I hurt him enough for him to die!" she cried back.

Gabriella and Donnie sleepily emerged from their room. "What's wrong, papa?" asked Donnie. "We heard shouting when we were sleeping."

The others exchanged worried glances. Abigail went to the children and gently told them, "It's alright, children. Go back to bed for now. We'll be sure to be quiet from now on."

Phillip paced the kitchen anxiously while Serena cried into her hands. Abigail looked between them helplessly, but thought it best to leave the farmhouse so that Phillip and Serena could speak privately. "I must leave now," she told Phillip. "But I will pray for the judge to be merciful."

Phillip nodded and opened the front door for Abigail. He wanted to say something, but all he could do was stand there in silence as he watched her leave the farmhouse.

When Abigail returned to her bedroom in the house, Ethan was trying to calm the crying baby. "Thank goodness you're here," he laughed. "I don't think he would have waited another minute."

Abigail calmed the baby, but began to whimper herself. Ethan looked worried. "What happened? Is Serena not coming to help?"

Abigail shook her head and answered sadly, "No. She won't be helping after all."

In a log cabin deep in the woods, William opened his eyes again, and quickly moved the quilt off of his body and onto the floor. He sat up in the bed and removed his jacket, feeling too warm to wear it. Greta Jenkins sat in a chair beside the bed and looked up at him. "It's about time," she said. "Are you ready to eat?"

William felt the sweat sliding down his face but was suddenly aware of how hungry he was. "Do you have extra food? I don't want to be any trouble."

Greta laughed and nodded toward the nightstand. "There's soup and bread there just for you."

William ate it gratefully and realized it was the first time in weeks he felt hungry. His fever had gone, but he worried that he was contagious to Greta. "I'm sorry I came here when I was so ill. I never meant to come into your home."

"It's no bother," she replied. "But you only seemed worried for your wife. Is she ill too?"

William looked alarmed. "I hope not!"

"Oh," she laughed. "Then why did you come to me asking for help?"

He sat there quietly, trying to collect his thoughts. "My wife Mary has been acting as the county midwife for months now, and the clinic in town is unable to take pregnant women. Mary is with child herself and I worry while she is out so much attending to births. Since you are a midwife…I thought…well, I hoped…"

"But what can I do about it? You know what the folks in town said about me. They don't want me attending their births anymore."

"What if I told them that it was a misunderstanding?

Or that the other doctor was only trying to squash the competition?"

Greta shrugged. "You could try, but I'm not sure what good it would do unless you made it a headline in the paper. That's what the last doctor did in order to ruin my reputation. Folks believe anything so long as it's in the paper."

"That's not a bad idea," William answered, thinking hard. "If I could get you a headline, would you resume your practice?"

"I suppose. Better than hiding out like a fugitive."

William laughed for the first time in weeks. "Then I'll call in a favor with a fellow I know at the editor's office."

"You will?" Greta still looked skeptical.

"You bet I will," he said. "Anything to help my wife get the rest she needs."

When William returned to his room at the clinic, he made a telephone call to the editor of *The Yorktown Times* and explained the situation.

"I see, I see," the editor said on the other line. "So, what do you want me to write?"

"I don't know," William chuckled. "You're the writer, Jack. I'm just the doctor. Maybe just tell folks that she is capable and that she has my support. That ought to do it."

"Sure thing, Dr. Hamilton. You might have called just in time for me to get it in tomorrow's paper."

"Great, thank you, Jack." William was satisfied when he hung up the phone with the editor, and noticed that he began to feel better with each passing moment.

In the servants' quarters of Davenport House, Nora was looking at Clara's dinner tray in confusion. "What's this?" she demanded.

"Miss Clara's dinner," answered Mrs. Malone.

"It looks like cornbread and chicken soup!" Nora shrieked.

"You're a smart one. With them brains, you might be able to help the detectives with their investigation."

Nora glared at her. "But I took this off the menu! Didn't you see that I wrote in chicken salad for tonight?"

Mrs. Malone shrugged. "I suppose I did see, but I thought Miss Clara would rather have this."

"I'm in charge of the menus now! Make the salad at once!"

Mrs. Malone defiantly plopped herself into a chair and began flipping through a magazine.

Nora's mouth hung open. "It's your job to prepare the dinner, now do your job!"

"I already prepared the dinner. If you want salad— make it yourself." Mrs. Malone sat back in the chair and relaxed.

"Listen here, you stupid cow—" Nora's rant was suddenly interrupted by Abigail clearing her throat in the doorway. "Oh, Miss Abigail—how may I help you?"

Abigail hesitated while she cast Nora a look of disapproval. "I wish to speak to Fiona. Please send her to my room."

"Right away, Miss Abigail," Nora replied. When Abigail left the kitchen, Nora began tearing lettuce and chopping vegetables for the salad. She placed it on a tray and ordered Jane to take it to Clara's room. "I'll deal with you later," she told Mrs. Malone. She then went to tell Fiona the message.

A few minutes afterward, Fiona entered Abigail's bedroom upstairs. "You asked for me, Miss Abigail?"

"Yes, I wish to speak to you for a moment," Abigail replied, closing the bedroom door. "But first tell me, did Mary eat her lunch today?"

"Yes, she did."

"Oh good," Abigail said distractedly. "That isn't why I called you up, though. I wanted to discuss your position here at the house."

Fiona looked at the floor. "I'm being punished."

"May I ask what for?"

"Miss Clara told Bridget to leave the house and not come back…but Bridget did come back and stayed in my room. I think it must be the reason for my punishment."

Abigail was quiet while she pondered the words. "It still does not make sense to me why Clara has made these changes, but it is her house, and she should run it as she pleases. Only, Sam told me he was worried about you."

Fiona looked up quickly. "Sam talked to you about me?"

"He asked me to intervene with Clara on your behalf, so that you might be reinstated as housekeeper."

Fiona felt her cheeks turning pink. "I'm surprised, Miss Abigail. I thought that Sam was cross with me."

Abigail was quiet for a moment, but finally said, "My brother cares for you a great deal."

Fiona could hear the racing of her own heart. "Did he tell you that?"

"He did not say anything," she replied with a smile, "but I can see it in his eyes. He said that you deserved better treatment than what Nora shows you in the servants' quarters. Are you happy being a housemaid here?"

"I'm grateful to have a job, Miss Abigail," she answered carefully.

"Ethan and I intend to move back to Philadelphia after the baby's christening. We will need a new housekeeper. I wondered if you would consider the position."

Fiona's eyes were wide. "You are generous, Miss Abigail. Thank you."

"I know it will be a drastic transition, so take your time to think about it and let me know when you have your answer."

Fiona nodded, then left the room quietly. Abigail changed into her nightclothes and lay in bed, consumed with thoughts about how she was going to tell Clara or anyone else about Serena.

In the servants' quarters, Jane returned to the kitchen with the tray of chicken salad for Clara. "Why have you brought that back here?" demanded Nora.

Jane flinched at Nora's tone. "Miss Clara said she was not in the mood for salad. She is asking for hot soup and cornbread."

Nora scowled as she served another bowl of soup from the pot that was still hot on the stove. Mrs. Malone snickered from the corner of the room as Nora clattered about the kitchen to make a new dinner tray.

Fiona had completed her duties for the day and hung her apron on a hook in the servants' lobby. She then quietly left through the back door and headed to the stable.

Sam was about to retire to bed when Fiona knocked on the door of his apartment. "Hello," he greeted her.

Fiona looked into his eyes worriedly. "I'm sorry about what I said to you before—about having anything to do with what happened to Mr. Collins. I know you couldn't have done such a thing."

"It's alright," he shrugged. "I figured you were upset about your sister and didn't really mean it."

Fiona swallowed the lump in her throat. "I've been afraid to ask what you meant when you said that I should ask her about what really happened that night. Do you think she was involved?"

"I don't know what happened that night, Fiona. I thought I heard something outside, and I looked out my window just in time to see Bridget running back to the house. I didn't want to get either of you in trouble, so I didn't say anything about it. She didn't tell you what she was doing out here?"

"No, she did not," Fiona answered with a heavy sigh. "I'm afraid. I don't know what to think!"

"I'm sorry," he told her. "I don't know what to think either."

Fiona changed the subject. "Your sister has been generous to me. She is making it possible for me to be a housekeeper again."

Sam smiled proudly. "I knew Abby could talk some sense into Miss Clara. That Nora is a tyrant. There's no way she's a better housekeeper than you."

Fiona hesitated. "I'm not going to be housekeeper of Davenport House anymore. Miss Abigail has offered me a position at the manor house when she returns to Philadelphia."

Sam looked distraught. "You're going with Abby to Philadelphia?"

"Well I think it would be ungrateful for me to turn it down. Your sister is so kind to me, and I suppose I have you to thank as well. She mentioned that you asked her to help me."

"I suppose I did," he mumbled, looking at the floor.

"I should get back to the house now. Thank you for your help. Goodnight, Sam."

"Goodnight."

Chapter 9

"Good morning, Madam," Nora greeted as she entered Clara's bedroom. "Look, our kind neighbor has brought these carnations for the parlor."

"Which neighbor?" Clara asked quickly.

"Mr. Blake."

Clara felt her heartbeat quicken. "Is he downstairs?"

"No, Madam. I told him you were in mourning and did not wish to visit with anyone."

"You should have spoken to me before giving such a message!"

Nora winced at Clara's reaction. "Forgive me, Mrs. Collins—do you wish to see Mr. Blake?"

"Actually, I do. Go run after him and bring him back to the house."

Nora looked at Clara with wide eyes, wondering if she meant it, but was not going to wait around to find out. She blurted, "As you wish, Madam," and hurried downstairs. Nora left through the back door where she was more likely to catch up with Joe Blake returning to his property. "Mr. Blake!" she called breathlessly.

Joe turned around, surprised to see the same maid who had just turned him away from the house. "Yes?"

"It's Mrs. Collins," she sputtered. "My Mistress wishes to see you after all. If you'll just follow me back into the house…"

Joe was bewildered, but replied, "Ah yes, thank you."

Clara checked her appearance in the mirror before going downstairs to meet with Joe. He was waiting in the drawing room when Clara entered. "Good morning, Mr. Blake," she greeted. "Please sit down."

" 'Morning, Mrs. Collins," he replied. Nora walked in with a tray just then.

"I thought you might like some tea, Madam," she said, pouring the tea carefully into cups and placing them on saucers. The room was silent while Nora served the tea to Clara and Joe.

"Thank you for the carnations, Mr. Blake," Clara said.

"You're welcome, Mrs. Collins."

Nora stood in the room and watched them both. Clara looked at her impatiently. "That will be all, Nora," she finally said.

"Oh—very good, Madam," Nora replied, picking up the tray and turning to leave the room.

Clara and Joe watched her leave. When Nora was well out of earshot, Joe whispered, "Clara, are you alright?"

"No, I'm not alright!" she answered frantically. "The police are coming to question me today. I'm afraid they will suspect me!"

"Tell them the truth, Clara. I'll back you up."

"How can I? It will make me look guilty for certain!"

Joe went silent while he remembered the night's events.

Clara looked at him worriedly. "Tell me it wasn't you who did it, Joe."

"It wasn't me!" he cried defensively, still attempting to keep his voice in a whisper. "You really don't know who might have done it?"

"No, and I didn't realize anything had happened to Lawrence until the next morning. I never even knew he had come home! Could there be a killer in this very house?" She covered her face with her hands. "I haven't slept in days!"

Clara jumped at the sudden ringing of the telephone. She and Joe were silent as they waited for the caller to be announced. Nora entered the room solemnly. "Telephone for you, Mrs. Collins. It is Chief Reynolds."

Clara's face went white. "I'll be right there," she whispered. Nora nodded and left the room. Clara stood up and held onto the sofa for support. "Oh Joe, I don't think I can walk to the library."

He came alongside her. "I'll help you. Just tell the truth, Clara. It might feel bad at first but it's better than lying to the police about something this serious."

She nodded weakly and held onto him as they made their way into the library. Joe helped her into the chair near the telephone and Clara trembled as she picked up the receiver. She motioned for Joe to listen with her. "Clara Collins speaking."

"Mrs. Collins, it's Chief Reynolds. I'm calling to say that we have a suspect in custody."

"You do?" she squeaked into the receiver. "Who is it?"

"I can only say that, at this time, we have a suspect who has confessed to the crime. We have many questions, of course, but we will not be coming to your home today after all."

Clara tried to catch her breath. "Alright, Chief," she said, her voice shaking. "Thank you for your call."

"I'll contact you again once we have more information," he continued.

"Very good. Goodbye, Sir."

"Goodbye, Mrs. Collins."

Joe looked at her in concern. "Do you feel better now?"

She breathed in relief. "Yes, I suppose I do. I can't wait for this all to be over!"

"I should be going now," he said, hesitating.

Clara swallowed her disappointment over him leaving. "Thank you for coming this morning."

"Of course. I hope the days get easier for you." He left Clara alone in the library and returned to his cottage on the neighboring estate.

Upstairs in Abigail's room, Sam was showing her the contract from Lawrence. "I need to get this straightened out with Miss Clara," he said urgently.

Abigail shook her head as she read the contract. "What a horrible man to have tricked you this way," she said about Lawrence. "I only worry that now is not a good time to speak with Clara. The police are coming to question us today, and it is tense for everyone. Do you suppose you could at least wait until after the funeral to talk to Clara about this?"

"Talk to me about what?" Clara said from the doorway.

Abigail turned to face her. "Oh, it's just that Sam wants to speak with you about the parcel of land he bought…but I wonder if he should wait for a better time."

"It's fine," Clara answered. "The police are not coming today after all. It's what I have come to tell you. They have a suspect in custody at the station."

Abigail raised her eyebrows. "Oh? Did they say who?"

Clara shook her head. "I'm just hoping we can put this whole investigation behind us so we may move on with our lives. Now Sam, what did you need to speak to me about?"

Sam showed her the contract. "This is what Mr. Collins told me to sign, but he made me think it was the deed that you had drawn up for me."

Clara became more angry with each word of the contract she read, and she tore the paper into pieces in front of him. "The land is yours, Sam. You may disregard anything that Lawrence might have told you. I will have the surveyor draw up another deed. Don't you worry about any of this."

Sam heaved a sigh of relief. "Thank you, Mrs. Collins." He left the room and Clara took a seat at Abigail's tea table.

Clara then blurted what she was thinking. "The more I find out about Lawrence, the more I despise him. How is a wife supposed to plan a funeral for a husband she hates?"

Abigail cringed and did not know how to answer.

Clara became apologetic. "You must think me a terrible wife for saying such a thing."

"I know you tried to be a good wife, Clara. Please don't blame yourself." Abigail thought carefully before she continued. "If there was more to be said about Lawrence and his dishonorable nature…would you want to hear about it?"

Clara shrugged. "I suppose it doesn't matter now. He must have been involved in something objectionable in order to lie to me about a sick mother. I found out that she died ages ago. Lord only knows what Lawrence was up to renting that room in Pittsburgh."

Abigail looked down at her lap while Clara spoke. She wondered if she should have said anything at all.

"Abigail," Clara said, looking at her curiously. "Do you know something about Lawrence that I don't?"

"I'm afraid so," she answered quietly. "But I don't want to hurt you more than you are hurting already."

"I never told you or Mary, but the truth is, I considered a divorce from Lawrence. I've felt terribly guilty for thinking that way, ever since he died. If you have anything to tell me now, perhaps it will not hurt so much as lessen this guilt I feel over wanting to be rid of him."

It was all the answer that Abigail needed. "Then I will tell you what I do know of him, but I must warn you that it is terribly unpleasant. I don't imagine you will feel much guilt after you hear what I have to say."

"Go on," Clara prodded her.

"Are you aware that Lawrence had a child with another woman?"

Clara's mouth hung open in shock. When she recovered enough to speak, she cried, "Of course I did not know! How did you find out?"

"I only learned of it yesterday, when I visited Serena Valenti. She has given me permission to speak of it now. I was aware that she had a child several years ago, but I never knew who the father was until now. Lawrence abandoned her as soon as he learned of the pregnancy."

Clara put her hand over her heart. "Serena Valenti? Good heavens! So that's why Lawrence treated her abominably when I introduced the two of them! He forbade me to have anything to do with the Valentis, but he made it sound like it was because they are Italian! I feel so angry right now!" She stopped to take deep breaths. "But I'm glad you told me. It's probably what Bridget came to the house to tell me that night. I still feel badly for sending her away. I suppose that hearing her out would have been better than never knowing the truth about Lawrence."

"But that was another matter entirely," Abigail said gently.

Clara was aghast. "You mean there is more?"

Abigail was about to speak, but Ethan entered the room just then, holding a newspaper in his arm. "Is Mary alright?" he asked in concern. "I didn't see her come down for breakfast."

"She must still be in her room," Clara answered.

"Ethan, will you check on her and make sure that she eats? I promised William," Abigail told him with urgency.

"Sure I will," he said, although he seemed hesitant. "Mary doesn't seem herself lately. I think something is bothering her."

"She hasn't seen William in months," Abigail replied sadly. "And she's been working so very hard."

"With any luck, she won't have to work like this for much longer." Ethan said, giving the newspaper to Abigail. She and Clara read the headline together while Ethan left to check on Mary.

Yorktown's Most Capable Midwife Returns!

Greta Jenkins was the county's beloved midwife before a jealous doctor schemed to end her practice. The conniving former doctor of Yorktown(who currently awaits trial for his other schemes) spread false rumors about Miss Jenkins, effectively ending her services as a midwife. It is now confirmed that Miss Jenkins was falsely accused all along and she is once more offering her midwifery services to expecting mothers throughout the county.

We welcome Miss Jenkins back with open arms as Yorktown's most capable midwife.

The Yorktown Times wishes to thank Dr. William Hamilton for bringing this story to our attention, and for his hearty recommendation for Miss Jenkins as the town's most capable midwife!

Abigail cringed. "I know that William was only trying to help, but I'm afraid this article does not show favorably upon Mary at all."

"Mary needs rest more than anything else," Clara remarked. "You know that nothing ever seems to print right in the paper."

Ethan entered the bedroom again. "Mary is still sleeping. I asked Fiona to take her a breakfast tray." He noticed that Abigail seemed weary as she finished nursing the baby and held him to her shoulder. "Do you want me to take him?"

"Yes, please," she said, holding out the baby for Ethan.

"We'll go out to the stable to see the horses so you ladies can talk." Ethan gathered some blankets from the bureau and headed out the bedroom door.

"Abigail, you were about to tell me something when Ethan came in with the paper," Clara reminded her.

"Oh that," she grimaced. "Bridget came to my room the night of the ball to tell me what she learned about Lawrence. Apparently, before he married you, he had an awful plan that he thought might trick me into being with him! Lawrence knew that my husband was sent to fight in the War, and Lawrence schemed to have me falsely notified of Ethan's death!"

Clara gasped in horror. "Oh no! Abigail—I'm so sorry!

What a wretched thing for anyone to do!" She rose from her seat and crossed her arms angrily over her chest. "I cannot believe I brought such a wicked person into this house! And now I want to die at the thought of him being buried in the family cemetery, near my mother or father. He deserves no such honor! I don't know how I will consent to it when the ground is ready!"

Mary appeared in the doorway just then. "I'm off to check on Mrs. Gerald," she notified them quietly. "I wanted to see that you two are alright first."

Clara managed a smile. "Mary, we are the ones who are concerned for you. Did you eat your breakfast at least?"

"I did," she answered, and looked in the empty cradle. "Where is my nephew?"

"Ethan took him out to see the horses," Abigail explained.

"Then I will be sure to kiss him goodbye before I leave," Mary said, stifling a yawn.

"Wait, Mary—I should tell you that the police have called. They have a suspect in custody," Clara said.

"Then I hope that justice is served swiftly for your sake, Clara. I'm sorry I cannot be of more help to you in your time of grief."

"You have nothing to be sorry for, dear. But when you do have a moment to talk, I would like to speak to you about all that has happened lately. For now, just take care of yourself."

Mary nodded. "Thank you, Clara. Good day to the both of you."

After Mary left, Clara turned to Abigail. "You look weary, yourself. I'll leave you to rest now."

Clara left the room, and Abigail lay back in her bed and closed her eyes. She opened them a short while later to see Ethan returning with the baby. He smiled apologetically. "Patrick is ready for you."

"Thank you," she replied sleepily. "How did he like the horses?"

Ethan smiled. "I can't wait to get him one someday. I'll tell him all about the time before automobiles and how we used to get around using only horses."

Abigail giggled about it and proceeded to nurse the baby for a few quiet moments while Ethan sat nearby.

Fiona came to the door shortly after. "I'm sorry to bother you, Miss Abigail. I was just so worried all of a sudden and didn't know who else to ask."

Abigail looked up in concern. "What is it?"

"Is it true that the police are holding a suspect at the station?"

"Yes, it is what they told Clara."

"Did they say who?" Fiona continued, wringing her hands.

"The police did not say who," she answered. "Why are you worried?"

Fiona looked nervously between Ethan and Abigail. "I'm worried that my sister might have been suspected."

"Oh," Abigail said quickly. "I don't think the police have Bridget. I have reason to believe it is someone else."

Fiona put her hand over heart. "Oh, thank goodness. I'm sorry for bothering you." She quickly left the room, and Ethan looked at Abigail quizzically.

"What's going on? Who have the police caught?"

"You should close the door," Abigail told him. "The others don't know yet. I wanted to tell you when I found out, but I'm having a difficult time coming to terms with it, myself. I went to visit Serena yesterday to find out when she would come to help with the baby. It is a complicated story, but apparently she was involved in Lawrence's death. She said she would turn herself in to the police today."

Ethan was stunned. "I can't believe this. I mean, I don't know her real well, but the way Valenti talked about her, she couldn't have hurt anyone. Valenti must be taking this hard…his family means everything to him. And jail is no place for a woman."

"It's a shock," she agreed. "I only hope this has all been a misunderstanding somehow, and that Serena may return home as quickly as possible." Ethan looked at her compassionately. Abigail managed a smile when he began to stroke her hair and look lovingly into her eyes. He leaned in to kiss her, but the moment was over quickly when Ethan sprang from the bed in alarm.

"What was that?" he cried.

Abigail's eyes were wide as she sat up in the bed. "It sounded like a gunshot." They both flinched as two more shots were fired, the sound echoing off the house. Then, silence.

"It sounded close," Ethan said. "It must've been Sam. I'll go check it out."

But as Ethan was on his way to the stable, Sam was on his way out with his rifle. "Did you hear where it came from?" Sam was asking.

"Sounded close to the house. I thought it was you."

"No, it wasn't me. Should we check with Joe at the ranch?"

"Probably should, just to make sure."

"Hello!" Sam called as they approached Joe Blake's cottage.

Joe walked out to greet them. "I suppose you heard the

shots. I had to scare off some coyotes that were trying to get to the sheep. They're gettin' desperate now."

"I thought I spotted one near the estate yesterday," Ethan remarked. "They must be coming out of the mountains. So long as it's all clear, I'm heading back to the house."

"See you, Ethan," Joe called after him.

Ethan walked back to the house while Sam stayed behind at the ranch to talk to Joe. Before going inside, Ethan froze in his tracks when he observed that Phillip Valenti was approaching him on the front steps.

"I'm sorry to bother you," Phillip said quickly. "I only wanted to make sure everyone was alright."

"We're alright. It was just the neighbor scaring off some coyotes."

Phillip nodded. "I see." In the awkward silence that followed, Phillip thought he should turn around and return to the farmhouse.

Ethan spoke up before he could leave. "The sound of gunfire nearly scared me out of my skin."

"Me too," Phillip agreed quietly.

"There's something I've wanted to say to you, only I didn't know how," Ethan continued.

Phillip looked away from him. "I'm listening."

"I'm sorry about your sister. Abigail told me."

Phillip nodded. "I'm sorry too."

"If you need help with the children or anything—" Ethan stammered, trying to get the words out. "—I hope you'll come ask us."

"That's generous of you," Phillip said with a nod.

"I used to think of you like a brother, you know. When I came home and found out that you were with Abigail, I started to think that you and everyone else were out to get me. I even thought it might have been you who sent the letter telling Abigail I was dead."

Phillip shook his head. "I swear, I didn't have anything to do with that. I hope you believe me. I thought of you like a brother too, and I thought if I didn't make it back—" His voice caught in his throat before he continued. "I hoped you would raise my children as yours."

"The truth is that a cruel trick was played on all of us. I found out who it was that sent that letter, and I realized how much hate I carried because of it. I couldn't tell if it was you who I hated, or myself. But I suppose all this time it can't have been easy for you either."

"No, it hasn't been," Phillip mumbled back.

"The fact is that Lawrence Collins arranged for that letter to be sent with malicious intent. He messed things up for all of us. But I want to get on with my life now without thinking those evil thoughts anymore. What I'm trying to say is, I want the hate that I carried to die with him."

Phillip was stunned at the revelation of Lawrence's involvement with the letter, but he nodded in agreement and shook Ethan's hand when it was offered.

"Don't forget to come to us if you need something," Ethan called over his shoulder before he disappeared into the house. Phillip started to head back to the farmhouse deep in thought. As the men parted ways, both felt as if a weight they carried had been lifted off their shoulders.

Later that afternoon, Clara was walking down the grand staircase when she observed that Mary was just returning through the front door. When Clara approached her, it was clear that Mary had been crying. "Are you alright, dear?"

Mary wiped the tears from her face. "I'm tired. I want to go to bed."

"Is there anything I may do to help?" Clara asked sincerely. "I want to be sure that you are getting enough rest, especially in your condition."

Mary stared blankly in front of her and answered in a low voice. "Then you'll be glad to know that I am not going to attend births anymore."

"What do you mean?"

"Haven't you heard? I am a failure. I was never meant to be a midwife, and now everyone in town knows it." Mary hurried up the stairs to hide away in her room before Clara could say another word.

At the police station in Yorktown, Serena was led to a jail cell after another round of questioning with the police. The guard gave Serena a pitiful glance as he slowly closed the door of the cell after her. The guard did not even bother to lock the cell before he left for his chair.

The police chief remained at his desk, furrowing his brow as he looked over the papers in his hand. Detective Mitchell eyed him curiously. "What's your take on that young lady?"

"I think she tells the truth to a fault," the chief muttered. "The only trouble is, the injury she described is not consistent with what we saw during the autopsy, and the location she described doesn't match where the men told us the victim was found."

"Could she have misjudged the location?"

"It's possible, but…I don't think she's the killer at all… despite her confession. She'd have to be much bigger and bolder to inflict the kind of damage we saw. No, I think the killer is still at large, and it's urgent that we keep on with our investigation tomorrow at Davenport House."

Chapter 10

The next morning, Clara went to Mary's bedroom to check on her. "Good morning, dear. Are you coming down for breakfast today?"

Mary lay in bed and weakly shrugged her shoulders. "You go on ahead without me."

Clara pulled up a chair beside the bed and sat down. "I don't want to leave you alone until you tell me what is bothering you. I've known you for years and seen you go through so much…never have I seen you this down."

Mary's chin trembled. "Did you read the paper yesterday?"

Clara heaved a sigh. "I did see it, Mary."

"So did everyone else in town. The mothers that I have been attending just told me they no longer require my services. They are switching to the other midwife, whom my own husband recommended above me. William doesn't believe in me anymore."

"Oh come now, Mary, you know that's not true. William was only trying to relieve some of the burden so that you could rest, surely."

Mary looked at her sorrowfully. "The damage is done. I'm humiliated."

Clara gave her a handkerchief. "I'm sorry, Mary. I know it made you happy to attend the deliveries…but you did work yourself too hard. You must think of the baby."

"I am always thinking of the baby, Clara. In fact, I think about the baby so much that it makes me frightened. I'm afraid that, when the times comes, I won't be strong enough to give birth. I've seen what those other women have gone through. What if I don't live through it?"

Clara took her hand gently. "You must be the strongest woman I know. More than that, you have so many people here who care for you and want to help. You are married to the best doctor the county has ever known. We all believe in you."

"I don't know that I believe in myself right now," Mary said painfully.

Nora entered the room just then. "Mrs. Collins, Chief Reynolds was on the telephone."

Clara's heart raced in her chest. "I'll be right down," she said, attempting to sound calmer than she felt.

"Oh, I have already spoken to the chief and hung up the telephone."

"What do you mean you spoke to him? What did he say?" Clara demanded.

"He said that he and the detective will arrive shortly to continue the questioning. I told him you were out of town…but Chief Reynolds said they will come anyway."

Clara gaped at her. "Why did you tell him that?"

Nora shrank back. "I thought you wouldn't wish to be questioned, Madam."

"You had no right to speak for me! What am I to do

when the chief comes here and sees that I have not left town? Or do you expect me to hide in my own house like a criminal?"

"I—I don't know, Madam," Nora stammered.

"Go downstairs and we'll discuss this later. And don't attempt to speak on my behalf to anyone ever again." Clara sighed in exasperation and Nora scurried away.

Mary was bewildered. "What was all that about? And why on earth is Nora acting as housekeeper? I've been meaning to ask you what happened to Fiona."

Clara covered her face with her hands. "Oh, Mary, it's all a mess! A mess of my own making, I'm afraid!"

"How do you mean?"

"I'm worried the police will think that I'm guilty of killing Lawrence. I didn't go back to my room the night of the ball…Nora saw me come into the house early the next morning through the servants' door. I asked her to be discreet about it, but she would not do so unless I let her be the housekeeper."

Mary was stunned. "But if you weren't in the house, where did you go all night?"

Clara stood up in a fluster and closed the bedroom door before she sat down again. "I was with Joe…at his cottage."

Mary's eyes were wide. "You were?" she whispered.

"Oh it was all very innocent, Mary. Only I didn't want anyone to find out that I, a married woman, spent the night at another man's house. After the ball that night, Joe put his coat over my shoulders and left the party before I could return it. I followed him to the cottage and we ended up talking in front of the fireplace for hours. I suppose we lost track of time, because the next thing we knew, the sun was coming up!"

"Oh dear, Clara! And Nora has been blackmailing you with the secret all this while?"

"It's not only her fault, it's my fault too. I was shocked about what happened to Lawrence…and afraid for my own reputation…I wasn't thinking straight when I agreed to Nora's terms. I feel terribly guilty for downgrading Fiona like I did. I have let everyone down."

"Now you must take the chance to make it right," said Mary. "Don't worry about what people will think of you. Just tell the police the truth."

Clara sighed. "I suppose I somehow feel better already, now that I have told you. I felt so guilty all this while! I even worried you might stop speaking to me."

Mary managed to laugh. "Not a chance of that. I will need your help when the baby comes, so you won't get out of it that easily!" Clara laughed too. She and Mary then spoke for hours to pass the time while they waited for the police to arrive.

At the police station in town, the guard was opening the door of the jail cell that was assigned to Serena. "You're free to go, Miss Valenti."

Serena looked at the guard in astonishment. "Are you—are you certain that I am free to go?"

"Ask the chief if you don't believe me," he said with a shrug. He led her to the chief's desk where she was given the handbag she brought to the station the day she turned herself in.

"I don't understand," she said quietly. "But I'm grateful if I am truly free to leave."

"We received new information today, and it checks out. The Pittsburgh police are on the lookout for the real suspects—two men who were business partners with Mr.

Collins. They must have gotten to him after your incident with the shovel."

"Oh," she said in relief. "I never thought I hit him that hard, but I knew I must pay the consequences if he was dead from it."

"We've talked to the prosecutor and they've decided not to press charges against you, Miss Valenti. But I should tell you not to leave town in case we have further questions."

"Yes, Sir," she said quickly. "Of course. I'll just be at my brother's home."

"That reminds me—your family is here to see you."

"They are?"

The chief nodded in the direction behind Serena and she turned around. Her breath caught in her throat and tears filled her eyes. She suddenly fell to her knees, reached out her arms, and whispered, "Angelina."

The little girl walked into her mother's arms and held Serena tightly around the neck. "Mama."

Giovanni stood by as he witnessed the little girl being reunited with her mother. Serena held on to her and looked up gratefully at Giovanni. "Thank you. I was afraid I'd never see her again."

"There's a car waiting out front to take you home," he told her.

"But how did you—?"

"Perhaps he can explain it all to you later, Miss Valenti," the chief interrupted. "For now, we've got a lot more questions for Mr. Salvatore before he can leave. He's turned up some things about Lawrence Collins that we very much want to hear about."

Serena held her daughter's hand and tried to lead her

outside, but the little girl ran to Giovanni and hugged his knees, appearing in no hurry to let go.

He gave Serena an apologetic look. "Sorry, I guess she got a little attached these last days." He turned to the little girl. "Go with your mama, now. I'm going to stay and talk with these men."

Angelina did not seem happy about leaving at first, but soon she was contentedly snuggled into Serena's lap as they began the long drive to the farmhouse.

At Davenport House, Sam was working under the hood of one of the cars when Abigail approached him in the driveway. "The police are coming to ask more questions," she told him.

"Alright," he mumbled without looking up.

"Have you spoken to Fiona lately?"

Sam looked up quickly. "About what?"

"Well I offered her a housekeeper's position at the manor house," she answered.

Sam continued tinkering under the hood and grumbled, "Sure, I heard all about it."

Abigail frowned. "I thought you'd be pleased. She'll be well respected as housekeeper there. I'll see to it."

"I only wanted you to talk to Miss Clara about getting Fiona's position back here."

"But Sam, it isn't my place to question Clara in her household decisions. It isn't my house."

Sam grunted and stood up straight to close the hood of the car. "I never would have asked you for help if I thought you would just take her away from here."

Abigail gazed at him compassionately. "I see. I didn't realize that—that was what you were asking for. You know,

Sam, you can come live with us at the manor house, if you wish."

"Thanks, Abby, but I need to get my own house built. I've already bought some of the materials so I can get started. It will just be a small cabin for now, but it will be enough."

"Does she know how you feel?" Abigail asked carefully.

Sam shrugged. "I guess there's no point in saying anything now." Abigail watched helplessly while Sam packed up his tools and returned to his apartment above the stable.

Later that night at the Valentis' farmhouse, Phillip heard a knock at the door and went to answer it. " 'Evening. Can I help you?" he said to the strange man.

"I'm the new detective in town," answered the man with a gruff voice. "I hoped I could talk to Miss Valenti."

Serena peered around Phillip to see who was at the door. "Hello Giovanni," she greeted.

" 'Evening, Miss Valenti. I came to explain more about what's happened."

"Please, come in," she said eagerly as she cleared a place at the kitchen table. "This is my brother, Phillip. Phillip, here is Giovanni Salvatore, the investigator I told you about."

Phillip shook his hand. "Pleased to meet you. My sister says you've been a real help. I didn't realize you were a detective."

"I wasn't until today," he replied with an incredulous laugh. "After talking to the police for a few hours, I guess they decided they wanted me working with them, and they swore me in right then and there."

Serena beamed. "Congratulations, Detective. Thank

you for bringing my daughter back. Now can you tell me where she has been all this while?"

"That's why I've come," he said, taking the seat across from Serena at the table. "Now before you get worried, I just want you to know that the girl was being well cared for…only it was a tricky situation. I checked into Angelina's father and found these business partners of his. Well, they were disgruntled business partners who Lawrence owed a lot of money to. They took your daughter, thinking that it gave them assurance of getting paid by him. But Lawrence ignored their demands."

Serena gasped in horror. "My Angelina was being held hostage?"

"Something like that," Giovanni answered. "It's why I wanted you to know she was well cared for before I explained. A sister of one of the men took care of Angelina in a house in the countryside…but the men wouldn't tell me where she was until I told them where to find Lawrence. I had no idea they would show up here and beat him to death that same night."

Serena shuddered, but felt relief at the same time. "Now I understand."

"When I heard that Lawrence had been killed, I thought it best to lay low for awhile. But then I heard that you were in jail thinking it was you who killed him. I couldn't believe it. I hurried to Yorktown with Angelina to tell the police what Lawrence's partners told me about that night. I'm sorry I didn't come sooner."

"I'm only glad that my daughter is alright, and that we are back together as it should be," Serena answered.

Giovanni hesitated for a moment before asking his next question. "And how is the little girl?"

Serena didn't have a chance to answer him before Angelina emerged from one of the bedrooms. She walked straight to Giovanni and climbed into his lap, hugging his neck tightly. He smiled sheepishly in response. "I'm glad to see she's well. I hope everything goes better for you from now on."

Serena could not help but comment, "You look so much different now than when I met you in the city. Today you seem quite cheerful."

He laughed. "Well, I don't suppose I've had a job I could feel proud of until now. I think it will turn out nice. I don't want to go back to where I was, working for the kind of people that I was. You were the only decent person who came to me, really."

Serena blushed. Phillip looked back and forth between them and broke the awkward silence. "Well, I thank you for getting all this straightened out," Phillip told him.

"I suppose I better get next door to explain to the ladies at Davenport House. There's more to the story that needs to be told."

"Thank you for stopping by and explaining," Serena told him gratefully.

Giovanni stood up from his seat, but Angelina still clung to his neck. "I suppose this one isn't so anxious for me to leave," he chuckled. He gently handed the little girl to Serena, who promptly put her back to bed.

"I'll see you to the door, Detective," she said afterward, leading him to the front door. Phillip went into the kitchen to wash the dishes from their supper.

"There's one more thing, Miss Valenti," Giovanni told her from the doorway. "I've been wanting to give this back to you ever since you gave it to me."

Serena was stunned when he handed her the envelope full of money. "But it's your payment. You've done so much to bring my daughter home. How can I take it from you?" She tried to hand it back to him, but he refused to take it.

"I don't need it, Miss Valenti." Giovanni held out his hand for a handshake, but Serena put her arms around his neck instead.

"Thank you again for everything. God bless you for all you have done. And please, if we ever meet again, call me Serena."

At Davenport House, Mary, Clara, and Abigail were having tea in the upstairs sitting room, all glancing nervously at the clock. "Perhaps the police changed their mind about coming today," Abigail suggested.

"To be honest, I wish we could get the questioning over with already," Clara was saying, but jumped when someone was heard at the door.

Nora entered the sitting room. "The detective is here, Mrs. Collins."

"Please send him up," Clara replied. Mary held Clara's hand while they waited for the detective to enter the room.

Giovanni seemed uncertain when he arrived to the sitting room and saw the three ladies. " 'Evening. I'm Detective Salvatore, and I'd like to speak with Mrs. Collins."

"I am Mrs. Collins," Clara told him. "And these are my friends. I would like them to stay during the questioning, if you don't mind."

"Your friends can stay if you want, but I should say that the news I have for you is nothing pleasant," Giovanni answered.

Clara sighed. "It's alright. My friends can hear anything you have to say to me."

Giovanni took a seat across from Clara. "Very well, then I will begin. I'm not here to question you, Ma'am. The Pittsburgh police have two suspects in custody who have admitted involvement in Mr. Collins' death. A trial date will be set for them very soon."

"Excuse me, Detective," Abigail said quickly. "What about the person being held at the police station?"

"That suspect has been released, and the prosecutor will not press charges," he told her.

Abigail heaved a sigh of relief. "Thank goodness. I am sorry I interrupted. Please, continue."

"The suspects were former business partners of Mr. Collins. The deeper I looked into Mr. Collins' history, the more I uncovered about debts and nefarious business dealings. I don't suppose you know anything about these things, Ma'am?"

"Lawrence was gone for months at a time. He always said he was attending to his ill mother, but I found out quite recently that it was not true at all. He received mail at a Pittsburgh address that I did not know he had. So I don't know the first thing about what he was involved in."

"I suspected as much. Mr. Collins had run up debts all over Pittsburgh. He was seen gambling on many occasions, and began planning a business for the illegal distribution of alcohol."

Clara's eyes were wide. "I had no idea of any of this!"

"I'm afraid there is more, Ma'am. This brings me to the most unpleasant aspect of this investigation…but the fact of the matter is, you are not the first Mrs. Collins."

Clara sighed. "Lawrence did tell me that he was a widower. Maybe it was the only truth he ever told me."

"I'm afraid that's not true, Ma'am. That is, Lawrence

Collins was never a widower. What he did was seduce different women in separate locations, and proceeded to marry them."

"I don't understand," she cried. "You mean Lawrence pretended to be married to these other women while he was married to me?"

"It's the other way around, Ma'am. It was you that he pretended to be married to, since he was still legally married to his first wife. Your marriage to him was never valid in the eyes of the law."

Giovanni sat back in his seat while the words sank in for the three girls, who remained in stunned silence.

Finally, Clara spoke, but it was barely above a whisper. "Is there anything else?"

"I suppose the final news is that the body of Mr. Collins will be sent to his legal wife for burial arrangements. I am sorry to have to tell you all this, Ma'am. I hope you may find peace in the days ahead."

"Thank you, Detective," Clara said quickly. "I believe I will be fine, now that I understand the situation better."

Giovanni nodded. "I hope so, Ma'am. If you have questions about anything, you can call us at the police station."

"Very good," Clara said. "Thank you for coming tonight."

Giovanni rose from his seat. "Goodnight, ladies."

After he left the house, Mary and Abigail exchanged shocked glances with Clara. "I'm sorry, Clara," Mary told her. "To hear this after all you've been through!" Abigail nodded in agreement.

"Don't be sorry," Clara replied. "I feel like a burden has been lifted from me all of a sudden. I feel like I may even be truly happy again someday. Oh, I am so glad the detective came tonight!"

Abigail smiled. "I'm glad you are taking the news so

well, Clara. You always knew something wasn't right about Lawrence. I suppose you have no reason to feel guilt over any of it now."

Clara relaxed in her seat and almost felt like laughing. "I feel a hundred times lighter. I'm glad you could be here with me to hear the news. What a mess! And I don't need to be a part of any of it anymore, thank goodness. I don't even need to think about a funeral!"

"No, you do not," Mary said, trying to be encouraging.

"We can start everything fresh now, and put this whole ordeal behind us," Clara said determinedly. They all sat quietly in the room, unsure of what to say next. Clara suddenly rose from her seat. "There is something I need to do. If you'll excuse me, ladies." Clara headed to the servants' quarters, quite unexpected by the maids. She arrived just in time to see Mrs. Malone sitting at the table with her arms stubbornly crossed over her chest. She was in the midst of an argument with Nora.

"I'm tellin' you, this is how Miss Clara likes it," Mrs. Malone was saying. "I'm not changing it!"

"You will change it if I change it on the menu! I run this house, and you will do what I say, you stupid fool!"

Clara was flabbergasted as she marched into the kitchen to face Nora. "Oh—good evening, Mrs. Collins," Nora sputtered, wondering if Clara had heard what she just said. Mrs. Malone and the others made themselves scarce.

"You should be ashamed of yourself for speaking to Mrs. Malone in that manner," Clara scolded her. "It was a mistake to appoint you as housekeeper. A mistake I have regretted ever since I made the change!"

"But Mrs. Collins," Nora began impertinently. "What about your secret?"

Clara shrugged. "It is no longer a secret, and I don't need your help keeping it anyway. If you want to continue working at this house, you may do so as a maid, on the condition that you apologize to the staff and show them the respect they are due. Otherwise, you should leave the house first thing in the morning."

Nora pouted as she thought it over. "Does this mean Fiona will be housekeeper again?"

"I hope it does mean that," Clara answered. "But I have yet to ask her."

Nora scowled. "Then I will pack my things and leave first thing in the morning." She stomped away to her room while Clara summoned Fiona, Jane, and Mrs. Malone in the servants' lobby.

"There are some changes in the house I would like to discuss with you all. The first is that Nora will no longer be under my employment. It was a mistake of mine to give her the position of housekeeper, and I hope you may all forgive my poor judgment."

The staff nodded with curious eyes as Clara continued. "Fiona, I would like you to be housekeeper again, if you are willing. You always exceeded my expectations and I regret that I ever took the position from you."

Fiona smiled shyly. "I would be grateful to be housekeeper for you again, Mrs. Collins."

Clara began to feel lighter than ever and managed to smile as she made her final announcement. "There is one last change to be made. I would like to be known only as Clara Davenport from now on. I hope to never hear the other name spoken in this house again."

The staff nodded in agreement and Fiona gladly answered her, "Very good, Miss Davenport."

Chapter 11

Early the next morning in the servants' quarters, Sam was having breakfast at the kitchen table before beginning his work for the day. He raised his eyebrows when Fiona walked in wearing her housekeeper uniform and holding a clipboard. "Fiona? What's happening?" he asked.

"Miss Clara said I'm to be housekeeper again," she whispered with a smile.

Before Sam realized what he was doing, he had stood up from his chair and hugged her tight. "Just as you should be," he said.

Fiona blushed when he let her go, but was eager to tell him the other news. "Nora is not coming back, either."

"I thought it felt better in here than usual," Sam laughed.

"I'm afraid it will mean that Jane and I must work longer hours until I can hire a new housemaid—I'll be quite busy."

"Makes sense," Sam replied with a nod. "When you're not too busy sometime, maybe you could meet me outside for an hour or two. There's something I want to show you."

"I'll see if I can steal away. After all the commotion upstairs, I imagine everyone will want a day to relax. It's a long story, but there won't be a funeral for Mr. Collins after all. And Miss Clara only wants to be called Miss Davenport from now on."

"Really? Alright," he said. "I gotta get to work now. I'm glad things are getting to the way they should be in the house, and that you got your rightful job back."

Fiona smiled. "Thank you, Sam. I'm glad too."

Later that afternoon, Ethan was tending to the horses in the stable. He heard footsteps approaching, then a meek voice spoke from behind him. "Um, pardon me, Mr. Smith?"

Ethan turned around to see Serena standing there, holding the hand of a little girl. Ethan smiled when he saw the two of them. "Abigail will be happy to see you are both looking so well."

She smiled bashfully. "I hoped to see Abigail today, but I didn't know how Clara would feel about us going to the house. Would you mind asking your wife to meet us here in the stable?"

"Sure, I can tell her," Ethan responded. He first leaned down to smile kindly at the little girl, who peeked out from behind her mother's legs. Ethan did not mean to stare, but he was struck by the familiarity of her appearance. "She looks just like—" he began to say, but stopped himself abruptly. He stood up straight and faced Serena, who looked at him expectantly. "She looks just like—her mother," he finished. "I'll get Abigail now."

Abigail was smiling proudly when Ethan entered the bedroom. "What do you think? I just finished it this morning," she said. She took Ethan's hand and led him to the bed where baby Patrick lay in his flowing white christening gown.

"You did great, Abigail," he remarked, scooping up the baby in his arms and kissing his forehead.

"I'm so pleased with how it turned out. It looks just like the gown my mother used to have for all of us, but I don't know whatever happened to that one."

Ethan was quiet and deep in thought as he carried the baby around the room. Then he suddenly looked toward Abigail. "I nearly forgot to tell you, there's—there's a surprise for you in the stable. I'll stay here with the baby while you go look."

Abigail laughed. "A surprise? You have me very curious now. Will you at least give me a hint?"

Ethan smiled. "The hint is: the surprise will make you very happy."

She laughed again and pulled on her boots and sweater. "Then I can't wait to see it."

When Abigail walked into the stable, she gasped suddenly to see that Serena was waiting there. "Oh my goodness!" she cried, running to hug Serena. "When Ethan told me a surprise waited for me in the stable, I never expected to see you! Why don't you come into the house? Are you alright?"

"I'm more than alright," Serena beamed. "There's someone I want you to meet." She reached out her hand to Angelina, who was hiding behind one of the haystacks.

Abigail held her hands over her heart as the little girl briefly came into view, only to hide behind mother's legs.

"This is my daughter, Angelina," Serena said gently.

Abigail blinked back tears of joy. "She is lovely."

"I thought it best that we meet you out here. I did

not want to upset Clara by coming into the house," Serena whispered.

"I understand. Thank you for coming with Angelina. My heart is so full, it could just burst!"

"I also wanted to give this back to you," Serena told her, reaching into her pocket for the envelope. "The investigator did not require the payment after all."

"It was generous of him," Abigail replied, taking the envelope gratefully. "I'll be sure to speak with Clara about you coming to visit us at the house. I have a feeling she'll be more agreeable to it than you might think."

Serena nodded with a smile. "We should be getting back to the farmhouse now. Thank you for everything, and goodbye, Abigail." The little girl turned to face Abigail and waved goodbye before leaving the stable with Serena.

Abigail returned inside the house and stopped by Mary's bedroom before she went back to her own room. "Mary?" she called past the open door.

"Come in," Mary answered quietly. She lay in bed and stared blankly at the wall.

Abigail sat beside the bed and looked at her in concern. "How are you feeling?"

Mary shrugged but did not say anything.

"Oh Mary, I wish you weren't taking this so hard. If you want to blame someone, you can blame me. I am the one who telephoned William and told him that you were working too much and needed help."

Mary looked up at her. "You did?"

"Yes, and I am sorry about how it all got printed in the paper. It certainly wasn't fair to you. But I wish you would understand how much we care about you and want you to be alright."

Mary sighed and continued to stare blankly. "Don't feel bad, Abigail. It's not your fault that I feel this way."

"Then what is it?"

Mary was quiet for a long time but tears began to roll down her cheeks.

Abigail looked on helplessly. "Is there anything I may do for you?"

"No. There's nothing you can do for me." Mary turned on her other side, away from Abigail. "I want to go back to sleep."

"I will leave you to rest," Abigail replied softly. She left the room and headed down the hall for her bedroom where Ethan waited with the baby.

He was confused when he saw Abigail looking upset. "What's wrong? I thought you'd be happy to see them."

She managed a smile. "It was a lovely surprise to find Serena and her daughter together. I'm very happy for them. The thing is, I stopped by Mary's room on my way here, and she is not doing well. I'm worried for her. I'm not sure if I feel right moving away just after the christening as we planned. Perhaps we should stay a little longer."

"It's up to you," Ethan told her. "I'm fine with staying here or going."

"You are?" she asked hopefully. "Would you be be agreeable to waiting until after Mary has the baby? Now that I've had one of my own, I see how difficult it can be to keep up without help."

"I can wait," he said, kissing the baby on the forehead before handing him to Abigail.

"Thank you, dear. I'm sure Sam will be glad to hear that we won't be moving right away."

Ethan looked at her quizzically. "Why's that?"

"It's just a feeling I have," she replied with a knowing smile.

Downstairs in the house, Fiona was gathering Clara's coat and hat. "I won't be gone long," Clara was telling her. "I'll just be next door. I—I am going to visit Mr. Blake."

"Very good, Madam," Fiona said as she helped Clara into her coat.

Clara hurried through the crisp afternoon air to reach Joe's cottage on the neighboring estate. Joe greeted her in surprise. "Clara—you look cheerful today."

She smiled brightly. "I have news to announce."

"Well come inside and have a seat by the fire, if you want."

Clara nodded and followed him into the cottage. "So much has changed since the last time I spoke to you here," she began.

"I'm just glad to see you looking happy. What's your news?" he asked, taking the seat across from her in front of the fireplace.

"Where do I begin? It's all so maddening. At least I am not required to plan a funeral for Lawrence, for I have discovered that I was never his legal wife! The police learned of his deceptions and fraudulent business dealings. His death was by the hands of his business partners who came to the estate that night, apparently. But can you believe that he was already married to another woman when I met him?"

Joe was bewildered. "I suppose he fooled everyone."

Clara sighed in exasperation. "I should have been furious when the police explained it to me, but all I could feel was relief that I could move forward with my life. It's as if I've awoken from a bad dream."

Joe stared at her and didn't say anything for a while.

Finally he broke the silence. "Makes sense. It's too bad you had to go through all of that though."

Clara gave a slight shrug. "I'd rather not dwell on the past anymore. I only want to look ahead to the future."

"I'm sure you will make the most of it."

"Thank you, Joe. I think I will." She smiled and rose from her seat, ready to be shown to the door.

"Oh—you're leaving already?" Joe asked.

"Yes, I must get back to check on Mary. I need to make sure she ate her lunch today. But I thought you might have been interested to hear that news."

"I'm very interested," he blurted.

Clara giggled. "Why don't you come to the house tonight for dinner?"

"Sure. Sure, I'll be there," he said as they stood in the doorway.

"Then I will see you tonight," Clara replied, and she turned to leave.

"Wait—Clara—" Joe said.

She turned to face him. "Yes?"

"Well, I could maybe kiss you goodbye—just as friends of course—you know," he stammered.

"Yes, you may," Clara answered him. But the way he held her and kissed her just then left Clara breathless. "Good Heavens, Joe! Do you tell all of your friends goodbye like this?"

He grinned. "No, I suppose you're the only one. I guess I just wanted to do that for a long time."

Clara's face was red hot with embarrassment. "Yes, well—I'll see you at dinner tonight. Goodbye, Joe."

"Goodbye, Clara."

Back at the house, Mary was lying in bed, still staring

blankly at the other side of the room. She was startled to feel a warm hand on her shoulder. "Sorry, I didn't mean to scare you."

Mary was overcome with emotion when she heard his voice. She turned to see William sitting beside her. "Oh— it's been so long since I've seen you!"

William hugged her tightly. "I know, I'm sorry. I wanted to come earlier, but I couldn't. How are you feeling?"

"I don't know how to answer that…" she replied painfully.

"How do you mean? Is the baby alright?"

"Yes, as far as I know."

"Have you been able to rest?"

Mary hesitated. "No one wants me as their midwife anymore."

"Surely that's not true," he said with a puzzled look.

"Is it any wonder after what you said to the newspaper?"

"Mary, I don't have any idea what you're talking about. I spoke to the editor about writing something, but I never had a chance to read it myself."

"It doesn't matter anymore," she said in defeat. "The county has a new midwife, and she will do better than I ever did. But I'm sure you know all about that."

William looked into her eyes. "I still don't understand you, Mary. I've been out of touch with everything lately. I—I had a bad case of influenza."

Mary's defeated expression turned to grave concern. "You did? Are you alright?" She reached up to touch his cheek.

"Yes, I got through it," he said, holding and kissing her hand. "But you'll have to catch me up on all that happened while I was away."

Mary's eyes filled with tears. "A mother whom I was

attending—she passed away right in front of me—and the worst part is, I still don't know what I did wrong!"

William lay down beside Mary in order to hold her. "I didn't realize you went through that."

"I thought you must have heard about it, and it was why you recommended the other midwife over me."

"I never intended to recommend anyone over you," he answered. "I should have checked before they printed it in the paper."

"I'm not worried about that so much anymore. I'm worried that a woman died while in my care. I've replayed the night over and over in my mind, but I can't think of what I could have done differently to prevent it."

William stroked her hair as she recounted the events to him. He gave her a handkerchief when she was finished. "Mary…dozens of patients in my care have passed on during this last outbreak. Even though I should be used to it, I do lie awake at night wondering if I could have saved them if I did something differently. I remember the first patient I ever lost, and how devastating it was afterward. It breaks my heart to know that you've been going through this while I was away."

"You've truly lost dozens?" Mary questioned.

"I'm afraid so."

"How do you manage?"

"I suppose I try to remember the ones that I've saved over the years. Fortunately, that number is much higher."

"How terrible that you've had to cope with loss on such a scale. I can't imagine. Does that mean I'm not meant to be a midwife?"

"I'm sure you're competent, Mary. I haven't had a

chance to tell you how proud I am every time someone tells me of another delivery you attended alone."

She managed a smile. "Thank you, William. So much has happened while you've been away. I can drive a car now, you know. By myself."

William laughed. "I'm impressed! You must take me on a drive sometime."

"Sure, if you want me to," she responded shyly. "You won't be embarrassed to be seen with a woman driving you around?"

He laughed again. "I would never be embarrassed to be seen with you. I'd love to have you drive me around. We'll give the townspeople something new to talk about."

"Alright then. Will you be able to stay for awhile?"

"I want to. The Red Cross sent more volunteers to the clinic while I was in quarantine. They are running it without me now, but I need to return eventually. The thing is, I'm worried that I might be gone for our daughter being born. I want to be here when it happens. I don't want to miss a single moment."

Mary sat up in bed. "Our daughter? Do you think we are having a girl?"

William smiled knowingly. "It's just my guess."

Mary grinned. "Mine too!"

"I missed you," he whispered, leaning in to kiss her. When Mary closed her eyes and kissed him back, she began to forget every worry that had been keeping her down for so long.

Downstairs in the house, Clara was returning from her visit with Joe. Fiona helped her out of her coat while Clara explained, "Please see to it that an extra place is set at the table tonight. I have invited Mr. Blake for dinner."

"Very good, Madam," Fiona answered.

"Now I must check on Mary. Has she eaten yet today?"

"Dr. Hamilton is upstairs with her now."

Clara gasped. "William has come home? Oh, this is perfect! Perhaps things will begin to feel like normal again!"

"Yes, Miss Clara." Fiona put the coat away while Clara looked at her thoughtfully.

"How are things downstairs?" she asked.

"They are busy, Madam. I hope to hire another house-maid as soon as possible."

"Yes, of course," Clara replied. "I do appreciate you tremendously, Fiona. Why don't you have a break before the dinner tonight? You may take some time to do whatever you wish for a few hours."

Fiona smiled gratefully. "Thank you, Miss Clara." After Clara disappeared into the library, Fiona went downstairs to her room and changed into her best dress. She pulled on her coat and headed out the servants' door for the stable.

Sam was glad to see her approach. "Hello," he greeted with a smile. "Why are you wearing your Sunday clothes today?"

"I'm on a break just now," she answered bashfully. "Miss Clara said I may have a few hours before dinner to do whatever I'd like."

"Oh—are you going somewhere?"

"I only came to talk to you, Sam. You said there was something you wanted to show me."

"Oh that—um—sure—" he stammered.

Fiona could tell he became suddenly nervous. "If it's not a good time, you don't have to now."

Sam looked into her eyes but did not say anything for a moment. Finally he snapped out of his daze and said, "Sure it's a good time. I want to show you now. Let me just saddle up the horses and we'll be on our way."

Fiona gave him a confused look. "Do you mean we are leaving the estate?"

"It's not too far, but it will be easier to get there with the horses."

She was hesitant. "But Sam—I don't know how to ride a horse!"

"You don't?" he asked incredulously. "We'll just take one horse then…so long as you don't mind things being a little cozy." He saddled one of the horses and explained to Fiona how to hoist herself onto its back. When she struggled with her boot in the stirrup, Fiona suddenly felt his strong hands around her waist, lifting her up into the saddle.

"Thank you," she whispered, feeling embarrassed. When Sam climbed on behind her and put his arms around to hold the reigns in front of her, Fiona understood what he meant by things being a little cozy.

It was a new sensation trotting through the fields. Fiona worried that she might fall off the horse and she gripped the horn of the saddle for dear life. Then Sam spoke into her ear. "Don't worry, you're not going anywhere. I've got you." Fiona relaxed a little but felt relief when they arrived at their destination. Sam helped her down from the horse and began showing her around.

"It might not look like much yet, but I can picture it all in my head how it's going to be," he told her.

A look of realization crossed her face. "Oh! This is your land!"

He smiled proudly. "Sure is. Those trees over there make up the property line, and it goes all the way through to that fence over there. Here is where I want to put the cabin…and the garden can be just that way. I'll get some fruit trees planted as soon as the ground's ready."

Fiona nodded and looked everywhere he showed her. The vision he presented was so picturesque that she could imagine it in perfect detail.

"So, what do you think?" he finally asked.

"I think it's lovely. I'm very happy for you," she replied.

"Does that mean you like it?"

Fiona nodded. "Very much."

He smiled contentedly as he helped her back onto the horse and then climbed on behind her. "Thanks for seeing it with me," he told her. They rode back in silence, but Fiona realized that she was not worried about falling off anymore. She almost felt disappointed when the stable came into view again, because it would mean that her first real horseback ride was over.

Sam helped Fiona climb down and proceeded to get the horse ready to lead into the pasture. When he did not say anything else to her, Fiona cleared her throat awkwardly. "Thank you for showing me your plans. I hope you have a good day." She turned around to head to the house.

"Wait, Fiona—can I talk to you for a minute?"

She turned to face him. "Of course."

Sam motioned for her to have a seat on a haystack while he sat on one across from her. He looked at her solemnly. "When Abby said she would take you away to the manor house, I got pretty upset. I'm glad you'll be staying here instead."

"Thank you. I'm glad about that too."

"I was upset about you leaving because, well you're my

best friend. I'm happy every time I see you. I didn't want to think about what it would be like here if you left."

"That's very kind of you, Sam," she said, feeling her cheeks turn pink.

"I'm not saying it to be kind, Fiona. I'm saying it because I love you."

Fiona held her breath and couldn't say a word. It did not deter Sam from resuming his train of thought.

"I've been wanting to show you the property—and hoping you would like it. I thought if you liked it, you might want to live there with me."

"I would like to," she whispered.

He looked at her hopefully. "Does that mean you'll marry me?"

Fiona nodded shyly, but wondered if her heart might burst with excitement.

Sam couldn't contain his grin. "Alright then. You just let me know if there's anything in particular you want done for the cabin. I really want you to like it."

She nodded again. "I'm sure I will like it."

Upstairs at Davenport House, Abigail was in her room with the baby. Ethan walked in just then with a tray of cookies. "Oh, thank you," Abigail said, eagerly helping herself to one. She noticed that Ethan had a twinkle in his eye and a mischievous grin.

"What is it with you? You look rather pleased with yourself like you have a secret," she teased.

"Who, me?"

"You can't shock me," Abigail said confidently. "I know all the house secrets."

Ethan gave her a wry smile. "You don't know this one."

Abigail laughed. "Then I will hope you will tell

me instead of strutting about the room like you own the world."

Ethan laughed too. "I just left the stable…where your brother was declaring his undying love for the housekeeper."

Abigail gasped. "Right in front of you?" she asked in amazement.

"No, of course not. They never even saw me. I was quiet as a mouse."

Abigail clasped her hands together in delight. "Oh, my dear brother and Fiona! I'll bet that they are married before the year is up. How wonderful!"

"You must try to look surprised when he tells you," Ethan said with a chuckle.

"Do you know what this means? Our baby may have two godparents now. It's always favorable to have two godparents instead of one," Abigail smiled, admiring the christening gown that hung from the armoire.

"Abigail," Ethan said quietly. "I've had second thoughts about all that."

She turned to face him in dismay. "What do you mean? You don't want to have the christening?"

"The christening is fine," he said, leaning down to pick up the baby and settling into the rocking chair. "I meant second thoughts about Sam being godparent."

"Oh," she frowned. "I believe him to be capable if anything should happen to us, especially if he will have Fiona's help. But I've not spoken to him of it yet, so if you are not agreeable to it being Sam…we can have the christening without naming godparents…or we can choose someone else."

"I already know who I want it to be," Ethan told her. "But I don't know how you'll feel about it."

Abigail raised her eyebrows in surprise. "Are they Catholic?"

Ethan nodded.

She sat down across from Ethan. "It's so rare that you speak up about these matters. I'm sure I'll be agreeable about anyone you choose. I suppose I never realized you might have someone in mind."

Ethan looked at her intently as he rocked with the baby in the chair. "I've been thinking about it for awhile. I'm sure Sam and Fiona would have been fine choices…but I think it should be Valenti."

Abigail stared at him speechlessly, wondering if she could have heard right. She finally swallowed the painful lump in her throat and whispered, "Are you sure?"

"I'm sure. Is it alright with you?"

"Yes."

Ethan stood up, still holding the baby. "Then I think I'll go over right now and ask him."

Abigail nodded and handed him an extra receiving blanket before he left with the baby. She then returned to the bed, deep in thought, and became startled by a knock at the door. "Come in."

Mary entered, smiling brightly. "Is my nephew in here?"

"You've just missed him," she giggled. "Mary, you look well. I'm glad to see that your color has returned."

Mary sat on the bed next to Abigail and said with great delight, "William is home."

Abigail's face lit up and she hugged Mary. "I'm so glad for you. How is he?"

"He is well," Mary answered happily. She stood up from the bed to see the christening gown hanging from the armoire. "You've done a lovely job, Abigail. I can't wait to see little Patrick in it!"

"When Ethan comes back with him, I'll show you how he looks all dressed up in it."

"I wanted to speak with you about that," Mary told her. "I wondered if William and I may go to the christening. Father Salvestro said that we may attend as witnesses, even though we are not Catholic."

Abigail was bewildered. "You have spoken with our priest?"

Mary smiled bashfully. "I've visited him on several occasions now. He was so helpful to me in a time of need. We are also making plans to assist the orphans at the convent."

Abigail smiled and shook her head. "And I thought I knew all the secrets of the house. You have surprised me, Mary."

"I'm also going to ask Clara if we might have your priest over for dinner sometime. I've told William all about him, and he is eager to meet him properly."

"How wonderful. To answer your question, Ethan and I would be honored for you to attend the christening."

"Then you can come help me pick out what dress to wear," Mary replied. "But first, I think I would like to eat. I'm starving!"

Fiona entered the doorway just then. "Oh, I'm sorry to interrupt, I'll come back later," she said when she saw Mary.

"It's alright, Fiona, I am just leaving for the dining room. Is lunch about to be served?"

"It is, Mrs. Hamilton."

Abigail turned to Mary. "I'll be down in a moment, you go on ahead without me," she said. Mary then headed out the doorway.

Abigail smiled knowingly at Fiona. "Well?"

Fiona was too embarrassed to look her in the eye. "Sam spoke to me. He showed me the building site for his cabin."

Abigail continued to look at her expectantly. "And? Are we to be sisters?"

Fiona blushed and nodded. "I wanted to thank you for everything, Miss Abigail. I'm grateful for the position you offered me at the manor house, but I will be staying here after all."

"Of course! I am so glad for you," she said, hugging Fiona and kissing her cheek. "But now that we are about to be sisters, you must begin calling me Abigail."

Fiona smiled shyly. "I'll try. But I don't wish to keep you from your lunch. Goodbye, Abigail." She left the room for the servants' stairs and was suddenly aware of the fact that she couldn't stop smiling.

At the Valentis' farmhouse, Phillip stood speechless at the front door when he opened it to Ethan holding the baby.

"I want to ask you something," Ethan said to him.

"Sure—" he sputtered. "Come in." Phillip cleared a space for Ethan on the sofa while Donnie and Gabriella eagerly looked upon the baby.

"He's so little," Gabriella remarked. "And handsome."

"Alright children, don't crowd my friend," Phillip told them. "Why don't you take the game to your room while the grown ups talk out here." The children obeyed, but sneaked another look at the baby before they left for their room. All was quiet in the sitting area for a moment.

"How's everything at the house…after that miserable business with the police?" asked Phillip.

"I suppose everyone is eager to move on and forget about all that."

"Makes sense," Phillip said with a nod. The room went silent again.

Ethan cleared his throat. "Did you know we are having a christening for the baby at your priest's house?"

"I suppose I heard something like that," he replied.

"That's what I'm here about. Abigail and I talked about who we want to be godparent for our son…I told her I wanted to ask you."

Phillip stared at him in silence, trying to find the words he wanted to say.

"It's alright if you say no," Ethan added slowly. "We can ask Abigail's brother."

"I want to do it," Phillip said quickly. "I'm honored that you want me to."

"Then I'll tell Abigail," he responded. "Do you want to hold him for a minute before I go back to the house?"

"Sure," Phillip said, carefully taking the baby into his arms.

Serena emerged from her room after putting Angelina down for an afternoon nap. She was stunned to see Phillip holding the baby while Ethan stood nearby. Phillip turned to Serena. "They're asking me to be godfather for this little one."

She tried to contain her surprise. "You must be honored, brother."

"I am indeed," he answered proudly. He handed the baby back to Ethan and led him to the front door.

They shook hands before Ethan walked away. Phillip closed the door behind him and leaned against it, clutching his chest. "I can't believe I got to hold him. I never thought I'd see him again."

"You will see him soon enough at the christening," Serena told him gently. She watched through the window as Ethan walked away from the farmhouse. "Do you think he knows?"

A feeling of peace settled over Phillip as he joined Serena at the window, and together they watched Ethan carry the baby away. "He knows."

CHAPTER 12

...six months later...

"Oh Sam, the cabin looks lovely!" Abigail cried in excitement.

Sam looked on proudly as he dismounted from his horse and helped her down from hers. "I can't take all the credit. Joe and Ethan helped me over the summer."

"Is it finished?"

"Just about. Come look inside," Sam told her, leading her through the doorway.

"Do you suppose it will be big enough?" she asked.

"We made it so we can add more rooms the more children we have."

Abigail giggled. "It's funny to hear of my own brother thinking of having children. Have you decided on a wedding date yet?"

"Not yet. Sometime when the house is done, I suppose."

"And will Fiona stay on as Clara's housekeeper?"

Sam shrugged. "I told Fiona she could stay home and

have babies all day if she wants to, but she wants to keep working at the house for now. How's your little one doing?"

Abigail laughed. "Ever since Patrick learned to crawl, he has been getting into everything. He certainly keeps Ethan and I on our toes. You'll see how it is someday."

"I guess we better get back now, but I'm glad you like the cabin, Abby." Sam helped her back onto her horse and they both rode back to Davenport House.

As Sam was putting the horses away in the stable, Abigail headed into the house where she nearly ran into Fiona. "Sam showed me the cabin," she said gladly. "It really turned out nicely!"

But Fiona did not seem to be listening. "Abigail," she said urgently. "Miss Mary is having her baby!"

Abigail put her hand over her heart. "Oh my! Has any-one called William?"

"Miss Clara called him just moments ago, but she's beside herself with worry!"

Abigail gave her a reassuring smile. "I'm sure every-thing will be alright. I will go attend to Mary."

When Abigail entered Mary's room, Clara was there pacing anxiously and wringing her hands. "Abigail! Thank goodness you're here!" she cried.

Abigail looked at Mary, who was grimacing in pain and breathing hard. "Oh dear, I think it must be getting close," she whispered to Clara. "She needs water. Why don't you bring some?"

"Oh! Right away!" Clara hurried out of the room and Abigail closed the door behind her.

She walked up to Mary and rubbed her back. "How are you?"

"It hurts more than I thought it might," she replied,

her eyes brimming with tears. "Does every woman truly go through this for a baby?"

Abigail smiled compassionately. "I'm afraid so. I know it's difficult, but you must try to relax as much as you can."

Mary nodded. "I'll try. I hope William comes in time. Clara said he was not at the clinic when she tried to telephone!"

"Don't worry about that just now, Mary. Try to relax."

Hours went by that Abigail attended her. Finally, she told Mary gently, "I'm sorry to leave you, but I must feed my son. Clara will sit with you while I'm away."

Mary whimpered in pain. "I'm afraid, Abigail. I feel like I will faint at any moment."

Abigail bit her lip nervously, but knew she could not wait much longer to feed the baby. "I won't be long, Mary. Have another glass of water and try to breathe through it."

When Abigail opened the bedroom door, she breathed in relief to see William running up the stairs toward her. "How is she?" he asked, but ran past her into Mary's room before she could respond. Abigail went to her own room, satisfied that William was now with Mary. Ethan was holding Patrick in the bedroom.

"How's Mary?" he asked.

"She's in labor for certain, but the pain will pass eventually," Abigail told him. She began nursing the baby, but could not shake the feeling that she had left Mary too soon.

In Mary's room, William rushed to her side. "Sorry I'm late. I was held up at a house call."

"I'm in terrible pain," she cried. "I don't think I can do this, William!"

"Of course you can," he said, looking into her eyes, and trying to get her to look into his.

When Abigail had finished feeding the baby, she suddenly cried out, "Ethan!"

He was startled and jumped from his chair. "What is it?"

She held out the baby to him. "Here, take Patrick. Something is wrong with Mary! I just had a terrible feeling." She hurried away and entered Mary's room in time to see William attempting to shake her awake.

"Mary!" he cried. His eyes were wide with fear when he turned toward Abigail. "Bring the smelling salts—she's unconscious!"

Abigail obeyed quickly and felt her breath catch in her throat when she observed Mary lying limp on the bed. "What else can I do?" she asked.

"I've just examined her," he replied, his voice shaking with emotion. "Her body hasn't progressed and she is shutting down. I'll have to remove the baby by Cesarean if either of them is to have a chance."

Abigail covered her heart with her hand, feeling the pain in William's voice. "I'll help," she said. "Tell me what you need me to do."

"I've never done this operation before," he answered her mournfully. "I need you to pray...get everyone in the house to pray that I can do this, and that Mary will live to see our child."

Abigail nodded solemnly and went out of the room to tell the others. When she returned, William was stroking Mary's hair and saying in a pleading voice, "I can't live without you. Stay with me."

Abigail put her hand on his shoulder. "She'll be alright. I have faith."

He buried his face in his hands. "I'm not sure if I do. I've never been this afraid to do anything in my life."

"William…I want to tell you that I've had dreams about our children growing up together, yours and mine. Mary is always in the dreams with us. She calls your little girl Violet. I know she will be well."

William moved his hands from his face and looked at her. "Has Mary told you about Violet?"

"It's only the name that she calls your daughter in my dreams. Mary has never mentioned the name to me."

William swallowed painfully before he spoke again. "We have to work quickly. I'm afraid of what might happen if we don't."

He and Abigail prepared Mary for the operation, hoping all the while that she would make progress before they started, but she remained limp on the bed. The sweat rolled off both their brows as they worked to control the bleeding. William soon handed Abigail the wailing baby, which she promptly wrapped in a receiving blanket.

William focused on attending Mary, and soon wrapped her with a bandage while Abigail calmed the newborn. "I've done all I can do," he whispered hoarsely.

"She will live," Abigail assured him. "You've done well."

"I hope so." He went to the washroom to clean up and returned looking weary.

Abigail felt sad for him. "Why don't you have a seat and hold your dear child while we wait for Mary?"

William lowered himself into a chair and gratefully took the baby from Abigail's arms. "She looks just like her," he sputtered, holding the baby close.

As the hours passed, everyone in the house waited in anguish for Mary to wake from her operation. Abigail observed that William fell deeper into despair with each passing moment, doubting his own abilities as his mind replayed the birth. Wishing she could alleviate William's sorrow, Abigail knelt beside Mary's bed and softly stroked her cheek. "You must wake, dear. We are waiting for you."

Mary's lips began to move. "It hurts so much," she mumbled.

Abigail quickly rose and took the baby from William so he could be by Mary's side. "Don't try to sit up, Mary."

Her eyes fluttered open and she turned to look at William. "You're crying. I'll try my best, but it hurts so terribly. I don't know if I can do it."

"It's already done," he told her gently. "It was all done while you slept."

"The baby has been born?"

"Yes," he answered.

"Did we have a girl?"

Abigail handed the baby to William to show Mary. "Don't try to get up, Mary. I will show her to you."

"Oh, she's lovely," Mary said weakly. "I wish I could hold her, but the pain is too much. I don't think I can move."

"Just rest for now," William told her. "You'll have plenty of time to hold her later."

Mary closed her eyes and breathed deeply as if she was drifting into sleep. Abigail left the room to tell those anxiously waiting outside the door that Mary was going to be alright. "She will need much help from us over the coming weeks," she explained. "Mary had an operation and it will take some time for her to recover."

"The poor dear," Clara replied. "Of course we will help

her! We won't let her lift a finger to do anything for herself for a long while."

"I'm glad she'll be alright," Ethan said. "You had me worried for a while there. Is there anything we can do for her now?"

"Why don't you bring our cradle into Mary's room? William could use a place to lay the baby."

William was grateful when Ethan entered with the cradle. "Thank you," he said, placing the baby onto the soft mattress.

"Is Mary asleep?" Ethan whispered.

William nodded and Ethan carefully kissed her on the forehead before he left the room. William sat beside her again and stroked her hair. Mary's breathing quickened and her eyes slowly opened again. "William," she smiled. "Have I dreamed it, or did you tell me the baby has already been born?"

He chuckled. "You didn't dream it. She is safely asleep in the cradle now."

"I'm sorry I couldn't manage it on my own," she said, her chin trembling with emotion.

William kissed her face. "You did wonderfully. Now all you need to do is get better."

"I'll do my best," she sighed. "Have you thought of what name to give the baby?"

He hesitated. "What name do you think?"

Mary looked into his eyes endearingly. "I thought that if we had a girl, we might name her for your dear little sister. What do you think?"

William felt the hair on his neck standing up and goosebumps covered his arms. "I think it is the perfect name for her," he whispered. "Thank you, Mary."

CHAPTER 13

"How are you feeling today, Mary?" Clara asked, peering into the doorway of her room.

"I am well, thank you," she replied cheerfully. "Violet is nursing so well now. Of course, William is taking splendid care of us."

"I'm glad to hear it," Clara responded. "Look what came for you today."

Mary smiled at the large bouquet of flowers that Clara held in front of her. "Who did they come from?"

"Joe," Clara answered. "I told him you had the baby and he gathered these from his own gardens."

"It was thoughtful of him," Mary remarked.

"He is very thoughtful...when he's not being utterly blind!"

Mary began to laugh, then winced at the pain. "Don't make me laugh...it hurts too much! Why do you say he is blind?"

"He kissed me once, you know. But he has never done so since! I give him every opportunity. I couldn't be more obvious that I want him to kiss me again. Sometimes I wonder if it's because I cut my hair short. He's been awkward around me ever since."

"Why don't you speak to him about it?"

Clara wrinkled her nose. "If he tells me that I am unattractive because of my hair, I think I would regret asking him at all. Men have no idea how difficult it can be to manage long hair, yet they seem to think that all women should have it."

"I suppose it was a bit shocking at first, but over the summer, I noticed several women in town with short hair. Perhaps Joe is only intimidated by you," Mary suggested carefully. "You are…outspoken. Men are sometimes intimidated by a bold woman."

"Well how else is anything to get done? We are so close to the vote now, Mary. I can feel it! I have every faith that we'll finally have it for the next election. But it will never happen for us unless we continue to speak out about it!"

Mary smiled at her. "I'll be certain to tell my daughter who to thank when it comes time for her vote."

Clara beamed. "It will be the most important change of the century. But what is so wrong with a woman having a mind of her own, and a voice of her own? I can't imagine altering my own convictions for the sake of pleasing a man. I tried it once before and it made me miserable."

"There's no reason to be miserable, Clara. I suppose I just mentioned it because Mr. Blake behaves shyly around you. The attraction between you two seems clear as day."

"Do you really think so?" Clara asked quickly. "Even after I cut my hair?"

Mary had to hold her stomach and stop herself from giggling. "Even since then. Why do you suppose he spends so much time with you, anyway?"

"We're good friends," Clara replied. "I can speak to him about anything, just the way I speak freely to you and Abigail. Well, almost anything. Clearly I cannot talk to him about this!"

Mary shrugged. "Why not?"

"Oh you are no help, Mary," Clara teased. "I'm going to ask Ethan if he'll find out what Joe thinks of me. Ethan and Joe have become rather chummy since they helped Sam build the cabin."

"Let me know how it goes," Mary said wryly.

Clara set the flowers in a vase beside Mary before she went down the hallway to peer into Abigail's room. Ethan was there sitting in the rocking chair with Patrick asleep on his chest. "Is Abigail here?" asked Clara.

"She went into town with Fiona. They are shopping for wedding clothes, I guess," he replied.

"Well it was you I wanted to speak to anyway," Clara said. "What do you think of my hair?"

Ethan groaned. "I don't know anything about girls' hair."

"Does the shortness make me terribly unattractive?"

Ethan glanced around the room for an escape, but Clara stood in the doorway of the room. "It's fine," he answered.

"Does Joe ever say anything about me? Has he said anything about my hair?"

Ethan searched his mind for an excuse to leave the room as quickly as possible, but Clara continued to look at him expectantly. He sighed in reluctance. "If there was ever a conversation about your hair, I sure don't remember it."

Clara turned to see Abigail approaching from the hallway. She moved to the side to let Abigail through the doorway, and Ethan wasted no time in finding an escape.

He handed Patrick to Abigail and fled down the hallway. Abigail was perplexed. "What was that all about?"

Clara sighed. "I suppose I asked him too many questions about my hair."

Abigail giggled. "That explains his sudden departure."

"Did you enjoy your shopping with Fiona?" Clara asked.

"It was enjoyable. In the end, Fiona decided that she would like to make her own dress. I am going to help her."

"I'll miss you when you move away again," Clara told her sadly.

"It's kind of you to say. Although, we have postponed our move so many times, perhaps you will be glad to see us go when we finally do."

"I don't see how I could be," Clara said, reaching toward the baby to stroke his cheek. "When this little one begins to speak, would you please have him call me Aunt Clara? I'm about to give up on ever having a family of my own. At least I might have some lovely children to call me aunt."

"What about Mr. Blake?"

"What about him?" Clara laughed. "He hasn't said a thing about his intentions for me."

Abigail raised her eyebrow. "Even if that is the case...I would not rule him out yet."

Clara looked hopeful. "Has he said something to you?"

"I've seen the two of you together—the way he looks at you when he comes for dinner—he doesn't have to say anything aloud for everyone to know that he admires you. No, Clara, if I were you, I would not rule him out yet." Clara smiled as she left the room with a newfound hope for the future.

At the stable of Davenport House, Ethan was saddling

his horse for a ride. Joe walked into the stable with his usual greeting. "Howdy, neighbor."

"Howdy," Ethan replied. "You need a hand with something?"

"No, I just thought I'd mosey on over for—well I suppose I don't have a good excuse," he said with a laugh. "I wondered about Clara. What do you think of her?"

Ethan groaned and wished he had finished saddling the horse two minutes earlier. "She's alright."

"She sure is," Joe replied. "Say, does she ever talk about me?"

Ethan shook his head in disbelief. "As a matter of fact, she just had me cornered in the house asking questions about what you thought of her."

Joe's face lit up. "She did?"

Ethan nodded.

"Well? What did you tell her?"

Ethan laughed and hoisted himself onto the horse before he answered. "I ran away. You'll have to tell Clara what you think of her yourself." And with that, Ethan rode out of the stable into the fresh autumn air.

He returned from his ride just in time to change for dinner. Abigail was in the bedroom and had already changed her clothes when Ethan arrived. "I'm going to put Patrick to bed in the nursery," she told him. "I'll be right down for dinner."

"Then I'll wait for you," Ethan said, putting on his tie.

"Oh don't worry about me," Abigail replied. "You go on ahead and I'll meet you there in a moment." She left the room with the baby and Ethan headed to the dining room.

Clara and Joe were just being seated at the dining

table. Ethan looked around the room. "Is William coming to dinner?"

"William is staying upstairs with Mary tonight," Clara answered. "Where is Abigail?"

"She's on her way now," Ethan said. "I hope."

They waited several minutes but Abigail did not come to the table, and the three of them sat there awkwardly.

"Well I suppose it will just be the three of us," Clara finally declared.

After another few minutes of silence, Joe cleared his throat and spoke up. "Sure is nice weather we're having."

"Yes. It is very nice," Clara agreed.

Ethan looked longingly toward the entrance, hoping that Abigail would come through at any minute. Then Clara turned to him purposefully. "Ethan, I wondered… what do you think of my hair, now that it is short?"

Ethan looked down at his plate. "Not this again," he muttered under his breath. When he looked back at Clara, she seemed to be staring at Joe for a response.

"It's nice," Joe said at last.

"Why thank you for saying so," Clara told him.

"How are your meetings in town coming along?" Joe asked Clara.

"Very good," she answered. "Although we will have a long ways to go with women's rights, even after we do get the vote."

"In what way is that?" questioned Joe.

"In many ways, not the least of which is that a married woman cannot even have her own bank account. Her husband has access to all of her money anytime he wants, but a woman has no such right to her husband's bank. It's not right that a man may so easily ruin his wife."

"I guess it might be alright if the wife trusted her husband to not do such a thing," Joe suggested.

Ethan wondered if either of them would notice if he got up to leave. He quietly lifted his plate and silverware from the table and decided to try it.

"Ethan, are you going somewhere?" Clara asked.

"Oh—I'm sorry—I just wanted to go check on Abigail—make sure she has some dinner. Also I think the two of you would like some privacy."

Clara was suddenly embarrassed, but Joe spoke up. "Go on then, Ethan," he said, stifling a smile.

Ethan gratefully left with his dinner plate and ran into Abigail just outside the dining room. She gave him an apologetic look. "Sorry I took so long. Patrick was not so eager to go to bed as I had hoped." She continued to walk past him toward the dining room.

"Wait, don't go in there," Ethan whispered. "Let's just go back upstairs."

"What do you mean? I'm feeling rather hungry," she replied.

"Here. This is for you," he said, holding his plate out to her.

Abigail gave him a puzzled look. "What's wrong? Why don't you want to eat in the dining room?"

Ethan groaned and continued in a whisper. "Joe and Clara are in there, and they're trying to put me in the middle of things."

Abigail covered her mouth as a giggle escaped. "Very well, we will go upstairs. But I'll need more dinner than your half-eaten plate," she added.

"I'll tell the maids to bring a proper tray," he

promised. "Maybe after tonight, those two won't be so bad to be around."

"Do you think Joe will finally speak up to her?" she asked with wide eyes.

"If he doesn't, you and I will take a trip away from the house until he does," Ethan joked. They made their way up the stairs, leaving Clara and Joe alone in the dining room.

The two ate in silence, even though each of them looked as though they wanted to say something to the other. Soon they were both staring at the empty plates in front of them.

"That was a fine meal," Joe finally said. "Thank you for having me."

"Yes, of course. Thank you for coming. I—I enjoy your company very much."

"I enjoy your company too," he said.

Clara rose from her seat and Joe did the same. "Did you get enough dessert?" she asked suddenly.

"Yes, I think I had plenty," he said, suddenly becoming shy.

"Do you want to stay for tea?"

Joe looked surprised. "Oh. Sure I do." But their tea time had less conversation than the dinner. After another round of awkward silence, Joe rose from his seat. "I suppose I should be getting back now."

"Oh. I will see you to the door," Clara said, placing her teacup and saucer on the table.

They walked together toward the exit that led to the gardens so that Joe did not have to walk around the outside of the house to get home. "Thank you again, Clara," he said quietly, looking into her eyes. He turned to leave, but Clara reached for his hand.

"Wait, please," she said. Her heart began to race when she felt him hold her hand and weave his fingers through hers. "I—I just wanted to know—" Clara stammered. "If you think I should wear my hair long again."

Joe was bewildered. "Do you want to?"

"Well, not really…I just wanted to know if you wanted me to."

"It's your hair," he chuckled. "You should have it how you want."

"Then—it isn't the reason you won't kiss me goodbye again?" she blurted.

"No, that's not the reason," he said, taking her other hand in his. "I didn't know if you wanted me to. I was worried I overstepped the last time because maybe you weren't ready to trust a man again."

"No, you did not overstep—I enjoyed it. I just worried because you never kissed me again after that. I thought it must have been because of something I did wrong, or it was my hairstyle, or the way I speak about politics."

"You don't need to worry what people think of that. You don't need to change for me or anyone. Then you wouldn't be you anymore—and you're the most interesting lady I know. I should never have called you an old spinster. Now I know there's a lot more to you."

Clara blushed furiously and hoped she would not have to give any more hints about what she wanted him to do next. She looked at him intently and said, "I trust you. And I don't want to be a spinster anymore." She closed her eyes and soon felt his lips pressing into hers with more intensity than the last time.

He pulled away slightly, whispering close to her face,

"I want to be with you and make you happy, if you want me to."

"Yes, I do," she answered quietly.

Joe opened his eyes and smiled, waiting for her to meet his gaze. "I promise I won't interfere with your bank or property or anything else. It'll all be yours, just as it is now."

Clara smiled back. "Thank you for being considerate… but I do trust you, Joe. I don't want it to be all mine anymore. I want it to be ours. There's just one thing I hope you'll agree to."

He laughed. "And what is that one thing, that I'm already sure I'll agree to?"

Clara beamed with joy as she answered him. "I want to have a big wedding—here at the house, with all of our friends present. I want it to be such a grand event that we will all think of it for a long time to come. It's what I have wanted ever since I was a girl, and I've waited for so very long."

"Then the planning can begin this minute," he replied with a grin. "I think both of us have waited to plan this day for long enough already."

DAVENPORT HOUSE
Hard Times

MARIE SILK

As Mary descended the grand staircase, she could see the new housekeeper pacing anxiously and wringing her hands by the front door. "What is it, Mrs. Spencer?" Mary asked her.

"Um—there's a lady here to see Miss Clara..."

Mary sighed. "Clara is not able to receive visitors."

"That's just it, Mrs. Hamilton. I told the lady that my Mistress was indisposed, but she would not take no for an answer. She kept asking questions about why Miss Clara would not see her."

"Don't worry, I will speak to the lady myself since I'm going outside anyway. I only hope it's not the journalist for that horrid gossip column." Mary wrapped her shawl around her shoulders and walked out the front door.

"Good afternoon," she greeted the woman who waited at the bottom of the steps.

The woman had gray hair pulled back into a bun and she stooped forward to balance on a thick wooden cane. Mary was perplexed at the way the woman seemed to stare at her. Mary pulled her shawl tighter around her shoulders as goosebumps covered her arms. She felt relieved when the woman finally stated her business. "I am here to see Clara."

"I am sorry, but Clara is indisposed today," answered Mary. "Would you like me to take a message to her?"

"What's wrong with her?" asked the woman quickly. "She's not ill, is she?"

Mary was taken aback that the strange woman would speak so boldly, but Mary was not about to give her any details. "Again, I am sorry, but as I say she cannot receive visitors just now. I am glad to relay any message you may have for her."

"No bother," the woman muttered. "I need to speak with her in person."

Mary nodded and tried to smile but felt increasingly awkward under the woman's intent stare. "Very well, Ma'am. If you'll just give me your name—I will tell Clara that you stopped by the house to see her."

The woman gaped at her. Mary felt more uncomfortable by the second and regretted that she had not just said goodbye and returned into the house. The woman's voice cracked as she responded emotionally. "Mary! Do you mean to say you don't recognize me? I am your mother!"

Introducing a very special look into the early years at Davenport House, when the stories of Mary, Clara, Ethan, and Abigail were just beginning...

DAVENPORT HOUSE PREQUEL

Debutante

MARIE SILK

The family saga begins in *Debutante*, a prequel to the *Davenport House* series. Life in 1909 America is explored from the perspectives of the wealthy Davenports and their servants, six years prior to the events of book one.

While her father is away on business, sixteen-year-old Mary Davenport feels confined and alone, despite her privileged life at the family's mansion. As the day of Mary's debutante ball draws near, her controlling mother attempts to separate Mary from her only friend, the lowly son of a servant.

In a Pennsylvania shantytown, a young girl is hired to make a gown for a debutante ball. She gives up her education so she may earn a wage to help her impoverished family. Neither she nor Mary is aware of how connected their futures are destined to become.

...coming soon...

About the Author

Marie Silk has enjoyed writing stories in many genres since childhood. She lives with her family in the United States and frequently travels the globe to learn more about the world and the people in it. Marie is inspired by history and the feats of humanity from ancient civilization to present day. She is the author of the Davenport House family saga.

For contact details, exclusive content, and information on upcoming releases, please visit: MarieSilk.com.